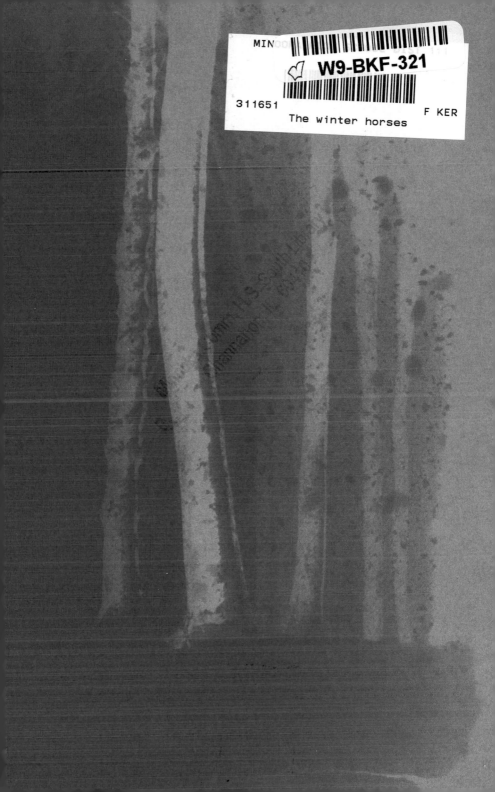

THE
WINTER
HORSES

THE WINTER HORSES

PHILIP KERR

Alfred A. Knopf 🐾 New York

Text copyright © 2014 by thynKER ltd
Jacket art copyright © 2014 by Eva Kolenko

All rights reserved. Published in the United States by Alfred A. Knopf, an imprint of Random House Children's Books, a division of Random House LLC, a Penguin Random House Company, New York.

Knopf, Borzoi Books, and the colophon are registered trademarks of Random House LLC.

Visit us on the Web! randomhouse.com/teens

Educators and librarians, for a variety of teaching tools, visit us at RHTeachersLibrarians.com

Library of Congress Cataloging-in-Publication Data
Kerr, Philip.
The winter horses / Philip Kerr.—First edition.
    p.   cm
Summary: "Kalinka, a Ukrainian Jewish girl on the run from the Nazis, finds unlikely help from two rare Przewalski's horses." —Provided by publisher
ISBN 978-0-385-75543-6 (trade) — ISBN 978-0-385-75544-3 (lib. bdg.) — ISBN 978-0-385-75545-0 (ebook)
1. Holocaust, Jewish, 1939–1945–Ukraine—Juvenile fiction. [1. Holocaust, Jewish— Ukraine—Fiction. 2. Jews—Ukraine—Fiction. 3. Przewalski's horse—Fiction. 4. Horses—Fiction. 5. Survival—Fiction. 6. World War, 1939–1945–Ukraine—Fiction. 7. Ukraine—History— German occupation, 1941–1944—Fiction.] I. Title.
PZ7.K46843Wi 2014
[Fic]—dc23
2013035978

The text of this book is set in 12.5-point Linux Libertine.

Printed in the United States of America
March 2014
10 9 8 7 6 5 4 3 2

First Edition

This book is dedicated to Naomi Kerr.

PRZEWALSKI'S: pronounced "shuh-VAHL-skeez"

MUCH OF THIS OLD story has been gathered together like the many fragments of a broken vase. The pieces do not always fit as best they might, and indeed it's quite possible that several of them do not belong here at all. It cannot be denied that the story has many holes and could not withstand much scrutiny. Historians will object—as they always seem to do—and say there is no real evidence that the old man and the girl who are the story's hero and heroine ever really existed. And yet if today you were in Ukraine and dared to put your ear into the wind or perhaps took a trip across the steppe and listened to the deep voices of the bison, the whoop of the cranes, or the laughter of the Przewalski's horses, you might learn that about the truth, the animals are never wrong; and that even if there are some parts of this story that are not exactly true, they *could* be, and that is more important. The animals would surely say that if there is one truth greater than all of the others, it is that there are times when history must take second place to legend.

I T WAS DURING THE summer of 1941 that, to a man, the management of the State Steppe Nature Reserve of the Ukrainian Soviet Socialist Republic ran away. Before he drove from the reserve in his shiny black limousine, Borys Demyanovich Krajnik, who was the senior manager, ordered Maxim Borisovich Melnik—who looked after all the animals on the nature reserve—to run away, too.

"The Germans are coming," he'd told Max. "Their armies have attacked and invaded the Soviet Union without warning. They've already taken the great city of Kiev and they will be here soon. Perhaps as early as next week."

Krajnik was emptying his desk and packing his bags while he was speaking to Maxim Borisovich Melnik and seemed to be preparing to leave.

"But I thought the Germans were our allies," said Max, for much had changed in Ukraine since 1919.

"They were, that's true. But now they're not, see? That's just politics. Doubtless they're after the oil fields of the Crimea. For their war machine. Look, Maxim Borisovich, all you need to know now is that the Germans are fascists and when they get here, they will kill you. Of course, in time our own Red Army will defeat them, but until this happens, you should definitely leave the reserve."

"But where shall I go?" Max asked Krajnik.

"That's your problem, Comrade. But my advice is to go east, toward our own forces. Go east as quickly as you can. However, before you can leave, there's an important order I'm giving to you. Very important. It comes from the central committee."

Max was astounded that the central committee of the Communist Party even knew he still existed, let alone that they had given him an important order. He couldn't help smiling at the very idea of this.

"An order for me? What is it, Comrade?"

"The committee orders you to slaughter all of the animals on the reserve."

"You're joking, Borys Demyanovich. Or perhaps the committee is joking."

"The central committee doesn't make jokes, Maxim Borisovich."

The smile disappeared from Max's old bearded face

as quickly as it had arrived. He rubbed his neck thoughtfully; it always seemed to hurt a little when the subject of killing an animal came up.

"Kill all our animals, you say?"

"All of them."

"What—the zebras? The ostriches? The llamas?"

"Yes, Comrade."

"Including the Przewalski's horses?"

"Including the horses."

"For goodness' sake, why?"

"To stop them from falling into enemy hands, of course. There's enough meat walking around this reserve to feed a small army. Deer, goats, bison, horses, chickens— they're all to be shot. I'd help you myself but, er . . . I've some important orders of my own. I'm urgently required in Kharkov. So I have to leave today. Now. As soon as I've finished talking to you."

"But I couldn't kill our animals, Comrade," said Max. "Some of them are very rare. So rare, their species might even become extinct. Not only that, but some of them are my friends."

"Sentimental nonsense. We're fighting a war, d'you understand? And our people are the ones who are facing extinction. The Germans mean to take our land and destroy all of us so that they can live on it. So, if I come back and find that you haven't carried out my orders, I'll call the secret police and have you shot. You've got a rifle. Now use it."

"Very well," said Max, although obviously he had no intention of killing any of the animals; besides, he rather doubted that Borys Demyanovich Krajnik was coming back anytime soon. "I don't like it, but I'll do as you say, Comrade."

"I don't like it any more than you, Maxim Borisovich, but this is a patriotic war we're fighting. We're fighting for our very survival. It's the Germans or us. From what I hear, they've already done some terrible things in Poland. So you would do well to be afraid of them."

And with those words, Krajnik drove away, as quickly as he could.

Max went outside the house and walked back to his simple cottage on the edge of the steppe.

The reserve of which he now had full charge was a hidden, enchanted place that consisted of a zoological park and an open territory of steppe covering more than three hundred square kilometers. A wild, desolate-looking region, it is mostly open grassland and largely treeless except for pockets of dense forest growing near rivers and lakes. The steppe is famous for being as bare as the palm of a man's hand, where there abides but rain and cold in winter and baking sun in summer, but in truth, the weather is more unpredictable than that.

Max did not think he would miss Krajnik very much. One of the reasons the old man was so fond of the reserve was that people like Krajnik were seldom encountered: there were just six small villages in the reserve and the nearest city, Mykolaiv, was more than three hours' drive away. Max thought that was just as well, since the whole idea of a nature reserve is to provide a sanctuary from men, where animals can exist without being put to work or hunted for food. In spite of what Krajnik had said about the Germans, the old man had high hopes of them being a real improvement on the Ukrainian Soviet government. And he did not think this hope was unreasonable.

For one thing, it was a German, not a Ukrainian or a Russian, who had loved animals enough to create the sanctuary at Askaniya-Nova. That same German—the baron Falz-Fein—had been the only man ever to show Max any real kindness. Everything he remembered about the Germans at Askaniya-Nova persuaded Max that if they did turn up and try to kill the animals, he could reason with them. After all, he could speak German, although it had been many years since he'd needed to. And so the first thing he did when Krajnik departed from Askaniya-Nova was not to shoot any of the animals but to return to his cottage and look for the German dictionary and grammar book that the baron had given him on his birthday more than forty years ago. And since he had only one small bookshelf with the Bible, a long poem called *Eugene Onegin* and *The Game of Chess* by Savielly Tartakower, Max quickly found these books and started to reacquaint himself with the complexities of the German language.

It was another two weeks before the German SS arrived in trucks and on motorbikes, and took over the main house. They seemed to be in a very good mood and behaved with courtesy when Max presented himself to some of the guards and asked to see the officer in charge. Despite the pirate skull and crossbones on their hats and helmets, they weren't at all frightening to Max. They ushered him into the baron's old study, where he snatched off his cap and introduced himself to a Captain Grenzmann. With his German improving all the time, Max explained that Askaniya-Nova was a nature reserve founded by a German baron, Friedrich Falz-Fein. The captain listened patiently and declared that he was fascinated with Maxim Borisovich's story.

"Was it the baron Falz-Fein who taught you to speak German?" he asked Max.

"Yes, sir."

"I thought so."

"It was here, as a matter of fact, that he taught me. But I haven't been in this room for twenty years."

The captain smiled. "I don't mean to be rude—Max, is it?"

Max nodded.

"But you have to admit it's amusing the way you speak German, as if you yourself were an aristocrat. I mean, it's amusing given the way you look. Indeed, if you'll pardon me for saying so, it's almost as if the swan was inside the ugly duckling."

"I hadn't thought of it like that, sir."

"What happened to him? To the baron and his family?"

"I think the baron is still living with his family in Germany, sir. But the old baroness was murdered by the Red Army. I myself was imprisoned and tortured because I had worked for them."

"And I suppose that's why you didn't run away. Because you knew you had nothing to fear from Germans."

"Yes, sir."

"And what do you do here on the estate?"

"I'm a sort of zookeeper, sir. Except that there are no cages or enclosures—for most of the animals, at any rate. One or two we keep in enclosures when we're trying to get them to breed. But most of the animals just roam around free, as nature intended."

Captain Grenzmann stood up and went to a framed map of the reserve that was hanging on the study wall.

"Show me."

Max pointed out the main features of the reserve and continued trying to ingratiate himself with the captain, if only for the sake of the animals at Askaniya-Nova.

"Well, thank you, Max. You've been most helpful. Not that it's any of your business, but we shall be here awhile, I should think. My men are tired and they badly need a rest."

"Well, sir, you've come to the right place, all right. This is a great spot to recuperate."

"I'm glad to hear it, Max. You know, we've been on the

go since June, without a break. The work has been most challenging. But this is the sort of ghetto that is more to our taste. Tell me, those three horses in the stables. Hanoverians, aren't they?"

"Yes, sir."

"Fine animals."

"You know your horses. Petrenko, the local party boss, often came here to ride with his daughter, sir. I used to groom for him. And to look after the tack for them."

"Perhaps you might do the same for me?"

"Whenever you like. You like to ride, sir?"

The captain allowed himself a small smile. "You could say that. I was on the German equestrian Olympic team, in 1936."

"That's wonderful, sir. You must be an excellent rider."

"Yes, I am. But not quite good enough to win anything myself. Still, Germany took all six golds, you know. Six golds and one silver."

"I'm not surprised, sir, knowing about Germans and horses. No one loved horses as much as the baron. It will be quite like old times, sir, having a German gentleman like yourself riding again at Askaniya-Nova. A real equestrian and lover of horses. That's grand, sir."

"I'm glad you think so."

"You know, it was the baron who first brought the Przewalski's horses here."

"These Przewalski's are the prehistoric horses, yes? The ones that can be seen painted on the walls of ancient caves by primitive Paleolithic men."

Max nodded.

"I believe I saw some of these horses at the Berlin Zoo, when I was a boy," said Captain Grenzmann. "As many as six."

Max nodded enthusiastically. "Yes, I remember them. We sold Berlin a Przewalski's stallion and mare. Berlin was very successful at breeding them. The last I heard, there were four Przewalski's in Berlin."

"You seem to know a lot about this, Max."

The old man shrugged. "I helped with the breeding program. First I helped the baron. And then the management of the State Steppe Reserve. The horses are very rare, you know. Perhaps the rarest horses in the world."

Captain Grenzmann laughed. "Perhaps. But if you'll forgive me for saying so, I think they're rare for a very good reason."

"It's true. They've been hunted to near extinction. Like the great auk. And they're difficult to catch."

"That's not the reason I meant."

"No, sir?"

"No. I rather imagine they're almost extinct because nature just wants it that way. It's survival of the fittest. You've heard of the phrase? What Charles Darwin says, about natural selection. In the struggle for life, some species and, for that matter, some *races* are simply stronger than others. So the strong survive, and the weak perish. It's as simple as that."

"Oh, the Przewalski's are strong, sir. None stronger. And they're clever, too. Resourceful. Cunning, even."

"Cunning, you say?"

"Like a fox, sir. Too cunning to be domesticated, sir. I suppose that's why I'm so fond of them."

"That's an interesting comparison. But you can't deny that they're also very ugly. And certainly inferior to those beautiful Hanoverian horses."

Max was about to contradict the captain, but the man smiled and raised his hand. "No, Max, please, don't say another thing. I can see we could stay here all day talking about horses, but I have a great deal of paperwork to do. Reports for my masters in Berlin on what my special action group has been doing for the last few weeks. So if you'll excuse me. I must get on."

"Shall I saddle the big stallion for you tomorrow morning, sir? His name is Molnija."

"Yes. Please do. I'll look forward to that."

MAX WAS NOT THE only person at Askaniya-Nova who was fond of the wild Przewalski's horses. A girl had been hiding in the woods at the edge of the steppe for some time, and although she had, like many girls, loved horses as long as she could remember, for some reason that even she could not easily have explained, the wild Przewalski's horses made friends with her. This was just as well since she had no human friends. Her family were all dead, and the few people who inhabited the scattered villages in the region drove her away from their doors because they were afraid—afraid that if the girl was arrested by the Germans, then they might also be arrested. The girl understood this and did not blame them for shunning her; she forgave them for it and told herself she would probably have done the same, although as this story proves, this was clearly not the case.

The girl's name was Kalinka. Her father had kept big Vladimir cart horses for his business, and she had made friends with them. But her relationship with the wild horses at Askaniya-Nova—she had no idea they were called Przewalski's horses—was different. She supposed it had something to do with their intelligence and their curiosity. These animals were unusually clever and possessed a childlike playfulness that she had never before seen in horses. And perhaps, as outcasts themselves, the horses saw something similar in Kalinka; at least that's what she imagined. It's a strange thing, the human heart, right enough, but that's just as true of horses, and wild horses in particular.

Kalinka had awoken early one morning, after spending the night wrapped in a ragged blanket under a cranberry bush, to find one of the horses—a mare—standing over her. Instinctively she knew that, although the horse was wild, the horse wanted to make friends.

"Hey," she said. "How are you? Are you after these cranberries? Help yourself. I've had more than enough of them. Too many, probably."

Kalinka sat up, stroked the horse's nose, and let the animal smell her, recognizing that horses can quickly tell almost all they need to know about a person from her scent. At the same time, this made her frown, for she recognized it had been a while since she'd had a wash.

"Maybe that's why you're not afraid," she said, stroking the mare's nose. "Because I must smell as much of an

12

outcast as you are. Maybe it's just soap and civilization that makes animals distrust humans."

She frowned again as her stomach rumbled loudly.

"Sorry about that," she said. "The cranberries are tasty enough, but they don't make much of a meal when you're as hungry as I am."

The mare nodded with what looked to Kalinka like sympathy.

"You wouldn't happen to know where I could get something to eat around here, would you?"

The mare nodded again, turned around, and looking back at Kalinka as if inviting her to follow, walked on and led her about a kilometer or two away to a blue-painted cottage beside a small lake. The mare sniffed the air carefully as though weighing if it was safe, and then uttered a snort that Kalinka took as the all-clear to approach the place.

The front door was not locked, and quickly Kalinka went inside and glanced around the one neat room.

"This is nice," she said. She especially admired a handsomely framed oil painting that was leaning against the wooden wall. It showed the veranda of a large white house with lovely garden furniture and flower beds and a beautiful lady in a long white dress. It reminded Kalinka of summers gone and—she hoped—summers yet to come.

"I dislike doing this," she said, taking some bread and cheese for herself and an apple for the mare. "But I dislike starving even more."

When she came out again, they both returned to the cover of the woods and ate the food she had stolen from the blue cottage. Previously she had stolen only from the Germans, which—given that they stole from everyone else—didn't seem wrong at all; but it was very dangerous, and Kalinka had no doubt of what would have happened to her if ever she'd been caught.

Later on, the mare introduced Kalinka to some of the other wild horses, and she spent the night sleeping between the warm bodies of the mare and her stallion as if she'd been their own foal.

"That was the best night's sleep I've enjoyed since I was at home," she told the mare and the stallion when she awoke. "Thank you. I'm grateful to you. My old coat and blanket are getting a bit threadbare, I'm afraid. The wind blows straight through the holes."

The stallion turned and galloped away with what seemed like indifference, but the mare stayed. And because Kalinka had nowhere else to go, she decided to keep the horses company for another day or so.

Which soon became one week and then two.

The wild horses didn't mix with the other animals at Askaniya-Nova, and a longer acquaintance with them revealed to Kalinka that they were very different from the horses she had known before. The first time that one of the wild horses chased and fetched a stick like a dog was a revelation to her. They loved to play hide-and-seek, and they were fond of practical jokes: she lost count of the occasions on which her hat was snatched from her head and made off with, or a handkerchief nibbled out of her pocket with a stealth that would not have disgraced a competent thief. In the few moments Kalinka tried to find some privacy in the bush or behind a tree, she often found herself disturbed by a horse playing peekaboo. It was at times like these Kalinka was convinced that the wild horses of Askaniya-Nova were almost capable of laughter. Which was more than she could have said of herself. She seldom smiled, and she never laughed. After what she'd been through, it didn't seem she had anything to laugh about.

Certainly, the horses were extremely vocal. The lead stallion made five basic types of sound—the neigh, nicker, whinny, snort and squeal—of which there was a wide range of subtle variations. After a while, Kalinka calculated that the horses were capable of making at least six different kinds of snort, and it was soon apparent to her that the horses could communicate with each other on what was a fairly sophisticated level. This enabled the small herd to work like a pack of dogs. Scout horses were sometimes dispatched by the lead stallion to look for better grass, and the same stallion quickly made the rest aware when his nose told him that wolves were close—although these knew better than to risk attacking the horses. This was hardly surprising, as Kalinka saw how the horses could be very aggressive with each other. She herself was bitten on a number of occasions—painfully, on the behind, when she bent over. She understood this was meant to be a joke, although it was not a joke she found very funny—and sometimes she was even kicked. Kalinka soon recognized that the wild horses were resourceful to the point of being devious: she saw them unlatch gates, steal food, ambush rival zebras and even count. The horses were extremely fast. They also possessed keen senses of smell, hearing and sight—much keener than her father's horses' and probably as keen as those of any wolf.

They were a little peculiar to look at, however. The mare who had first befriended Kalinka was no more than one and a half meters high at the withers and had a thick, short neck and a low-slung belly. The head and the curved, almost semicircular neck were darker than the horse's body, and a dorsal stripe ran from the stiff, brushlike mane along the broad back to the tail. She possessed no forelock. Her muzzle was pale and the strong legs striped like a zebra's, but the most striking difference from the domestic horse that Kalinka noticed was the short-haired, almost furry tail, which was more like a fox's brush or a sable's pelt. Kalinka soon formed the opinion that this strangely furry tail helped explain the wild horse's demonstrable cunning.

TIME PASSED, BUT THE Germans stayed and, like everyone else, Maxim Borisovich Melnik learned after all to fear them. They shot many of the estate's deer, goats, ducks and geese—even some of the llamas and camels—and ate them, but that was not the reason why Max learned to fear the soldiers. He feared the Germans because from time to time they would receive orders to perform "special police actions" and a group of them would drive grimly away from Askaniya-Nova, returning a few days later, falling-down drunk, with a crazy look in their blue eyes, sometimes hysterically laughing and trembling with adrenaline, their weapons still warm to the touch and always spattered with blood.

On the rare occasions Max went to one of the villages on the estate and spoke to the peasants who lived there—these days they feared the Germans more than they feared the Soviet secret police, the dreaded NKVD, and hence they no longer felt inclined to shun Max—he heard stories of the unspeakable things that the SS captain and his men had done, of thousands of people murdered and then buried in mass graves, and of whole towns put to the torch, and he shuddered that he would have to go back to Askaniya-Nova and be near such inhuman monsters.

The villagers urged Max to flee Askaniya-Nova, but always he went back because he feared for the animals. And for this reason, it was Max who pointed out the weakest deer and fowl for the soldiers to shoot for their pot. As for the llamas, he'd never been that keen on them: llamas spit. It's one thing being bitten by an animal; it's quite another to be spat upon. Max had never gotten used to that, just as he could not get used to the idea that Captain Grenzmann could allow his men to behave with such callous barbarism when he himself was a man of some refinement. As well as being a captain and an Olympic equestrian, Grenzmann was an artist of considerable skill; his pen-and-ink drawings of the Hanoverian horses in the stables were among the finest pictures of horses that Max had ever seen. Oddly, however, the Hanoverians were the only subject that Grenzmann seemed inclined to draw. One day, while helping the captain mount Molnija for his morning ride, Max summoned up his courage and asked him about this.

"Why don't you draw one of our other animals, sir?"

he asked. "The European bison are very interesting, I think. Or perhaps the Przewalski's horses. I'd be interested to see what such a skilled artist as yourself might make of them."

Grenzmann gave Max a withering look—which was even more withering from the back of such a tall horse as Molnija.

"I'm not in the least interested in any of the other animals," he told Max. "Especially not your mongrel subhorses. In fact, I'm still wondering what we're going to do about those slitty-eyed beasts. Before we leave."

"Are you leaving, sir?"

"We'll have to before very long. The war isn't going well for us in this part of the world. Your Red Army is less than a hundred kilometers away. And we risk being encircled if we stay here. Chances are we'll have to fall back on Kiev before very long."

Max did his best to contain his delight at this latest news.

Soon after this conversation, Grenzmann gave Max one of his better drawings as a present, and every time the old man looked at it, he marveled that an artist of such great sensitivity should be capable of such diabolical cruelty. More importantly, he worried over just what the captain had meant when he had spoken of "doing something" about the Przewalski's horses.

The snow came early that year, cooling everything into a frigid silence. All of the lakes froze solid, each turning a different color: one was green, one was violet, one was silver, but the largest lake was black, with ice as thick and hard as a piece of pig iron, and almost as soon as Max broke through to the dark water with a hammer and chisel, it became ice again. Covered with a perfect blanket of thick snow, the endless steppe reflected the azure blue sky so that it resembled a petrified ocean on which no boat sailed. Forests of fir and birch froze as silver as Max's beard, and everything—Max most of all—seemed to hold its wintry breath. The old man sensed that something bad was going to happen at Askaniya-Nova and that it was going to be up to him to stop it somehow but, at the same time, he knew he was just one man against many; while he was a crack shot with a rifle, he could not resist a whole battalion of German soldiers. So he hoped and he prayed, and meanwhile he bowed and scraped before the handsome young captain and, every morning, saddled the big stallion as usual.

Max had to admit that the German was an excellent rider. The captain was a different man on a horse: he was patient and understanding and sufficiently relaxed in the saddle to always get the best out of the animal. It was plain to see why he had been picked for an Olympic equestrian team. To watch him ride a horse was to observe a perfect partnership between man and animal. Sometimes the captain put his face against Molnija's nose and talked to him as if he were a lover, and he always brought the horse a little treat—an apple, a carrot, or a couple of sugar lumps.

One day in December, Captain Grenzmann said to Max as he sprang up into the saddle, "*Molnija*. Does it mean anything, Max? Or is it just a name like Boris or Ivan?"

"It means 'lightning,' sir."

That seemed to please the captain, for he smiled and patted Molnija's neck fondly.

"How very appropriate," he said, and when Max looked baffled, he took hold of the collar badge on his greatcoat and leaned toward the old man.

"Are you blind as well as stupid?" he said. "This SS badge. It's supposed to resemble a double lightning flash. I wish I'd known this before. Really, Max, it was most remiss of you not to mention it until now. You know, I've a good mind to have you shot."

Instinctively, Max let go of the reins, snatched off his cap and bowed gravely.

"I'm sorry, sir," he said. "Really I am. You're right. I should have mentioned it."

But the captain was laughing. "I was only joking, Max," he said. "Lighten up a little. Don't be so serious."

"Oh. I see." He tried to smile, but this just looked like he was showing his teeth, which were sharp and yellow, and the tall horse backed away from the old man suddenly, as if he was worried that the old man was going to bite his withers.

"Steady, boy," said the captain, adjusting his seat. "Easy, Molnija." And mistaking the reason for the horse's display of nerves, he added, "I wouldn't really have him

21

shot. Not old Max. Not after all the faithful service he's given us."

"Thank you, sir."

"His mangy, substandard, rootless horses, on the other hand. They're a very different story."

"What do you mean?" asked Max.

"Didn't I say before? The Przewalski's are now proscribed—a forbidden breed—and as such are to be destroyed."

"You can't mean that."

"I'm sorry, but it's not up to me, Max. In all matters of race and species, the SS Main Office makes the decisions. And I'm afraid that, in the case of the Przewalski's horses, Berlin has ordered me to complete the work that nature has started, Max. To remove from the animal population of the Greater German Reich what is, after all, a biologically unfit species, in order to protect the line of decent domesticated horses—like Molnija here—from possible contamination by your wandering pit ponies. It's all part of our eastern master plan for the destruction of Ukrainian and Asian culture so that you people can be properly Germanized. Really, you should welcome this, Max. After all, the way you speak, you're almost a German yourself. Perhaps not to look at. I'll grant you that. Your appearance leaves a great deal to be desired. You're almost as ugly as those slitty-eyed, steppe-wandering nags of yours."

Max started to protest, to say that what Berlin had

ordered would be a crime, but then he stopped and re-minded himself that the extinction of a rare species of horse—compared to all the terrible crimes against hu-manity that Captain Grenzmann and his men had already committed in this part of Ukraine—might not count for very much in the eyes of anyone who wasn't a zoologist or, like Max himself, someone who just loved Przewal-ski's horses for themselves.

"A couple of specimens are to be shipped to Berlin," continued Grenzmann, "so that Reich Marshal Göring can hunt them on his estate at Carinhall. He's quite a collector himself, you know. But the rest of the Przewal-ski's horses are to be rounded up and shot here without further delay."

"Sir, it's not their fault that they're almost extinct. It's ours. Mankind's. If it wasn't for us, there would still be substantial numbers of these horses in existence."

"Look, there's no point in arguing about this, Max. The decision has already been made. Tomorrow we start the process of eradication."

The captain rode off.

MAX SPENT ALMOST THE whole night awake, wondering what to do. He sat in front of his fire, smoked several pipes and stared into the flames, asking himself what the baron would have done if he had been there. As a German aristocrat who was used to being obeyed, the baron would probably have reasoned with the captain; possibly he might have persuaded the SS captain that Germany had effectively lost the war and that there was little point in adding yet another terrible crime to his country's already ignominious account. The captain might have listened, too; the baron was a very persuasive man. But Max was not the baron, and try as he might to think of something, he finally concluded that really there was nothing he could do. Nothing that would have worked anyway.

He knew it was hopeless even to try and round up the horses and lead them to a place of greater safety; previous experience had taught him that catching even a Przewalski's horse that had gone lame could be the work of several frustrating days. A few of the horses—Ruslan, Mykola, Dmytro, Leonid, Ihor, Yaroslava, Snizhana, Oksana, Sofiya, Yulia and sometimes Luba—would come to Max's call when he had a treat for them, but they would never consent to being stroked, let alone consent to a rope or a bridle. Usually, it was possible to catch the horses only when they were very young and lacking in cunning and when they had yet to develop their tremendous capacity for speed. One of the two lead stallions, Temüjin, and his mare, Börte, Max had only ever seen at a distance. And it wasn't as if all of the horses were in one herd; there were two, perhaps even three, herds of about ten horses each, with one dominant stallion.

Max told himself that all of this was in their favor.

They were also able to survive a long time without water, which meant that their human hunters were denied the most obvious strategy—to hide by the lakes where the horses came to drink. Besides, the lakes at Askaniya-Nova were frozen, so that was good, too. Max himself had seen how a lead stallion would scout the way ahead to water before directing his herd with snorts and whinnies—sometimes from the cover of a bush or a clump of trees. The fact was that even on the reserve, where until now the Przewalski's horses had lived in almost perfect safety, the animals took no chances where humans were concerned.

Another thing in favor of the horses was that they

were stealthy at night—as stealthy as any fox—and, by day, astonishingly adept at using features of the country as camouflage. From what Max had read about the horses in books the baron had lent to him years ago, it was not unusual for Mongol hunters to track a small herd and then lose it, only to find out later on that the horses had been hiding close by all along.

Max concluded it was one thing for the German captain to say that his men were going to round up thirty Przewalski's and shoot them, but it was quite another actually to do it.

He fell asleep in his chair and dreamed sweet dreams of Askaniya-Nova before the Nazis and the Communists, and of the baron, who had been so kind to him.

A couple of hours later, he awoke with a start, certain that something he heard had interrupted his dreams. He stayed seated for a moment or two, his old ears straining to find an explanation for his sudden wakefulness.

And then he heard it: the sound of automatic gunfire.

Max grabbed his coat, his cap and his rifle, and opened the door. He listened again and, hearing yet more shots, he set off in the direction they had come from.

Any other man wearing a dirty fur coat might have been worried about being mistaken for one of the horses the Germans were probably shooting at. But Max cared nothing for his own safety; he welcomed any bullet that would have spared the life of one of his beloved Przewalski's, and he hurried toward the scene in the hope that he might still reason with the Germans.

Gradually he heard the sound of engines as well as automatic gunfire, and another ten or fifteen minutes' quick march brought Max to the brow of a small hill overlooking a wide, gently sloping snowfield, where a terrible sight greeted his eyes: he saw an SS motorcycle roaring across the steppe, and then another. The snow hardly interfered with their speed, thanks to their thick, knobbly tires. Wearing heavy leather coats, steel helmets and goggles, both riders were in hot pursuit of a herd of Przewalski's, and that would have been bad enough, as wild horses don't much care for noisy engines, but attached to each of the motorcycles was a sidecar in which another SS man was seated behind a heavy machine gun mounted on the chassis. These men were firing the guns in short bursts of five or six shots, but worse than that, they were grinning widely.

Several horses were already dead, and even as Max watched with horror, he saw another—a mare, he thought—falter in the midst of her frantic gallop, as if tripped by some unseen wire, hit the snow headfirst and then lie still.

He shouted at the four Germans to stop, but it was useless; they wouldn't have heard him anyway. For a brief moment, he considered shooting at the men with his rifle—he might have done so, too, but for the fact he knew he wasn't the type of man to shoot anyone. Killing an animal was quite hard enough, but killing another human being struck Max as something abhorrent.

So he just stood there and forced himself to watch.

Many terrible things had happened to Max in his life, but nothing he had ever experienced compared with the dreadful scene he was witnessing now.

Finally, when the horses were all dead or had escaped, one of the motorcycles turned around and drove back toward the old man. For a long moment, Max thought they were going to shoot him as well, but at the last minute, the man driving the motorcycle stopped, cut the engine and climbed off his vehicle. The other man stayed put, and Max was now near enough to see the smoke trailing from the long, air-cooled barrel of the machine gun that had been used to such deadly effect.

With a machine pistol slung around his neck, the driver walked solemnly toward him, lit a cigarette and smiled.

"Hey, Max, you want to be careful wandering around in that old brown fur coat of yours," said the man, whom Max had talked to before. "We almost mistook you for one of the horses and shot you, too."

"I wish you had."

"Don't say that. Look, Max, none of us wanted to do it—to shoot your horses. But orders are orders, eh? It's war. What can you do? The captain says jump, and we jump. That's how it's got to be." He offered Max the cigarette, but the old man declined with a shake of the head. "For what it's worth, none of the horses suffered. You get hit with a bullet from Hitler's buzz saw and it's over in just a few seconds."

Max nodded. "Did many horses escape?" he asked hopefully.

"A few. But we'll catch up with them later. We'll let them regroup and go after them again tomorrow, probably."

Feeling quite sick, Max wiped the tears off his old face and walked away without another word.

J UST AS HORRIFIED BY what had happened to the wild horses of Askaniya-Nova was poor Kalinka, for after living with them for several weeks, she had grown very close to these animals. Indeed, since her own family was now no more, Kalinka regarded the horses as a sort of substitute for brothers and sisters. And while she was astonished that anyone should have tried to exterminate a whole herd of harmless wild animals, she was hardly surprised that the authors of this crime should have been wearing the same gray field uniforms as the men who had killed almost everyone she knew in her hometown of Dnepropetrovsk.

Hiding in a thick grove of trees near the old man's blue cottage, she watched with horror as the Germans on their big, powerful motorcycles and sidecars chased the horses across the steppe, firing their machine guns and laughing like they were on some kind of macabre holiday. What was so funny about killing something, or someone? It had been the same back in Dnepropetrovsk, where the SS had gone about their bloody business with great good humor; indeed, it had seemed to Kalinka that many of them had been quite drunk, and she suspected the same was probably true of these men on the motorcycles.

Of course, Kalinka wanted to run out in front of them and tell the Germans to stop, but she knew they would not have listened to her. Back in Dnepropetrovsk, several girls not much older than Kalinka—including her elder sister Miriam's best friend, Louise, who was generally held to be the most beautiful girl in the city—had actually knelt down in the streets and begged the laughing Germans to stop what they were doing. They had been shot without mercy. So Kalinka stayed hidden and, with her stomach knotted, waited for the massacre to end.

Her hopes rose a little when the old man from the blue cottage arrived on the steppe, waving his arms and shouting loudly at the Germans. She hoped they would pay attention to him, if only out of respect for his silver beard, but they ignored him and carried on shooting. Kalinka almost hoped he might unsling the rifle he carried and shoot a few of them instead, although she could easily see how useless that would have been. The Germans had no more respect for old age than they did for youth; hadn't her own great-grandmother been shot—a woman

31

aged ninety-five? But still, she admired the old man's courage, for it was plain that they could have shot him just for the pleasure of it and because killing was all they seemed to know.

When finally the shooting stopped and the Germans drove back to the big house, where they were all staying, Kalinka waited for the old man to leave, too, before she quit her hiding place in the trees. She had learned to avoid all people, much as the horses did. Besides, the old man looked rather frightening.

Venturing out onto the steppe to see if she could help any of the horses who had been shot, she could soon see plainly that her mission was pointless. The Germans had done their job with predictably brutal efficiency, for the wild horses were quite beyond anything that even a veterinary surgeon could have done. A horse in motion is a beautiful, almost fluid thing, but now their ragged brown bodies lay on the pinkish snow like untidy heaps of solid, upturned earth. Nothing ever looks quite as dead as a dead horse. It was a heartbreaking sight.

To Kalinka's relief, there was no sign of the mare who had first befriended her, nor the stallion who was her mate; of course, this was no guarantee that they were still alive. The steppe is a vast plain and it was not unlikely that their dead bodies lay several kilometers on the other side of the horizon, where they might have been chased by the relentless SS motorcycles. But she hoped for the best, and it was with a tremendous sense of relief that when she returned to her hiding place, she found the stallion and the mare hiding there.

"Thank goodness you're alive," she said, embracing the mare. "I thought you were both dead."

Kalinka tried to embrace the stallion, too, but he was having none of it, and to have tried more than once would have been to risk a kick or a bite, so she embraced the trembling mare again, and this time she found there was blood on her hands.

"Oh, but you're hurt," she said, and as soon as she had found the wound—which was in the mare's shoulder—she scooped up a handful of snow with which to wash it clean and, she hoped, to stanch the flow of blood. Kalinka held the snow over the wound for as long as her bare hand could take the cold, and the mare seemed to appreciate her attempt to help, for she dropped her nose onto Kalinka's neck and licked it. But the flow of blood from the horse's shoulder was only a little diminished by the snow poultice.

Kalinka debated out loud what to do. "It's not like I can put a bandage or a tourniquet around this," she said. "For one thing, it would have to be a very big bandage. And for another, I can't see how it would possibly stay on. Stitches would be best, I think, but I've never done that kind of thing before. Besides, I don't happen to have a needle and thread."

She thought for a moment, and nodded firmly as she arrived at a decision:

"I think we'll see how you are in the morning and then, if you're still bleeding, I shall have to return to that old man's cottage and see if I can't steal a needle and thread. Although having seen his clothes, I don't hold out much hope of that. I never saw such a ragged-looking person. Except perhaps myself, of course. But then I've got an excuse. He's living in a warm cottage with a fire and a wood-burning stove, and I'm living out here, on the steppe. I'm sure if I lived in such a nice little place, my clothes wouldn't look like a family of mice had been nesting in them."

THE FOLLOWING DAY, MAX heard more gunfire in the distance, but this time he did not go and watch what was happening, nor did he go to saddle Molnija for the captain; instead, he stayed in and around his little blue cottage and tried not to think about what was happening. He washed his crockery, took out the hot ashes, did some dusting and swept the floor. A couple of times he caught his dog, Taras, looking at him in a strange way as if he held all men—including Max—responsible for what the German soldiers had done to the Przewalski's horses.

"What could I have done?" Max asked Taras. "You tell me. I'd like to know. Really, I would. The Germans would have shot me, for sure. And then who would look after you, dog? Tell me that? And, after all, it's not like the horses are the only animals at Askaniya-Nova. There's all sorts of rare breeds that'll need our help before this war is out—you mark my words. We'll recover. You'll see. The Germans can't stay here forever. You heard what Captain Grenzmann said; the war is not going well for them, so God willing, they'll be leaving soon. After they're gone, things will get back to normal. I promise. It'll be you and me and the animals, just like it was before."

The day after this, things were even quieter, but still Max did not go to the stables to saddle Molnija for the captain.

"He can saddle his own horse from now on," he told the dog. "I'll have nothing more to do with the Germans. Not if I can help it. I don't care what they do to me."

Taras wagged his tail as if he agreed with his master and went outside, for there was a new and interesting smell in the air. After a while, Max thought he might take a walk outside, too. On other days, he might have remarked upon the beauty of the reserve, but now all he could see was how harsh and unrelenting life could be. The sun bounced off the snow and dried his lips until they cracked and felt like the skin on his feet, while even the hairs in his ears froze solid in the icy wind.

Inevitably, his footsteps led him to the part of the steppe where he had seen the two SS motorcycles hunting down the horses.

About halfway there, he decided he would cut off the tails and bury them, since he knew he could not have mustered the strength to bury the horses themselves. But when he arrived at the scene, he found the bodies of the horses were gone, and the only things there to remind him of the terrible event he had witnessed were several circles of bloodstained snow.

"Where have they gone?" he murmured. "I don't understand. If there were any wolves about, they'd have eaten them here, surely. But there's not so much as a shinbone left."

Max was still wondering what had happened to the corpses of the dead horses when Taras lifted his muzzle into the air and barked loudly.

"What is it, boy?" asked Max, and sniffed the air. "Smell something different, do you?" He raised his face into the bora wind and sniffed again; only very gradually did his nose catch what Taras's keener sense had detected: it was the smell of fresh meat being cooked.

Almost immediately, Max guessed the true fate of the dead Przewalski's horses: the Germans had taken them back to the kitchens in the big house so that they might eat the meat for dinner. The worst part of it was that the smell was succulent and delicious and opened up a hole in Max's stomach as he suddenly realized just how hungry he was. It had been quite a while since he had eaten meat. Game was always thin on the ground in winter.

Max swallowed uncomfortably and stared at Taras.

"Well, go and get some grub if you want," he told the dog. "I shan't stand in your way or even blame you. There are some who say that horse meat is very tasty, but I shan't ever eat it myself. I don't think I could swallow the stuff even if I wanted to. I tell you, dog, it would stick in my throat and choke me."

A little to the old man's relief, Taras stayed put and then followed him back to the humble cottage. They were still en route when Captain Grenzmann overtook them on the back of Molnija.

"Good morning, Max," he said. "Isn't it a beautiful day?"

"I've seen better."

Max kept on walking, and with a quick, expert squeeze of his legs, Grenzmann urged Molnija a few paces ahead, then turned the stallion in front of the old man and his dog so that they were obliged to stop.

"Max, hold up there," said Captain Grenzmann. "Wait a minute, please. Where are you going?"

"Home," said Max dully.

"Yes, of course." Grenzmann jumped down off the horse and then drew the reins over his head. "Well, stay a minute, please. If you will."

"Say your piece," grunted Max.

"I've missed you this last couple of mornings. In the stables. We both have." Grenzmann patted the horse's flanks. "Haven't we, boy? I was never much of a groom, you know. I've almost forgotten what you're supposed to do. It's not the same without you there."

"Well, there's no great mystery about that," said Max. "I expect you know very well why I haven't been there."

"Yes, I suppose I do. But look here, Max, I didn't have much choice in the matter. Not after my superiors in Berlin made up their minds. I tried to explain this to you the other day. I'm just a captain, not a general. And I don't make policy decisions in such matters. I just execute them."

"It makes no difference what you are, out here," said Max. "You're the man in charge." He shrugged. "And it seems to me that we've always got a choice. I think that's what makes us human. Any man who says he hasn't got a choice about something might as well admit that he's not much better than Molnija here, with a bit in his mouth and a saddle on his back."

"Molnija?" For a moment, Grenzmann looked puzzled. "Oh, you mean Lightning, don't you? I didn't say, did I? Yes, I've renamed this horse. In the circumstances, I thought that was appropriate."

Max frowned. "I can't say I hold with giving animals new names any more than I hold with killing them for no good reason."

"Look here," said Grenzmann. "Please don't take that lofty tone with me. I rode out here to make sure that there are no hard feelings between us. In the same spirit of conciliation, I should like to invite you to come to dinner tonight."

"To eat my own dead horses? I don't think so, sir, thank you kindly."

"Max, Max." Grenzmann sighed. "Be reasonable. We could hardly let all that fresh meat go to waste. There's a war on, don't you know? Good meat is in shortage.

There are people in this part of the world who are starving. Besides, horse meat is much better for you than beef or pork. Did you know that? Back in Germany, we make a very popular sausage—*Rosswurst*—out of horse meat."

"If you'll forgive me for saying so, Captain, it's my sincerest hope that you and your men are soon back in Germany, eating some of that delicious-sounding sausage."

And with those words, Max walked away, followed closely at his heels by Taras.

Captain Grenzmann mounted the stallion and came after the old man.

"Well, I'm very sorry to disappoint you, Max, but I don't think this is going to happen; at least not for a while longer anyway. My battalion is cut off from our own lines, you see. By the Red Army. We're encircled in this reserve of yours. And until our own forces can break through to us, we're stuck here at Askaniya-Nova. Perhaps until the spring. So you'll have to put up with us for a while longer."

This was unwelcome news to Max—doubly so in the current circumstances—but he said nothing and trudged on.

"Anyway, if you do change your mind about dinner tonight, just come along. I can assure you, you'll be very welcome in our mess. I don't mind confessing to you that my men would feel a lot better if you were there. It's been troubling them, what happened here yesterday and the day before. They're all good boys, you know. With good hearts." With a hard snap of the reins, Grenzmann brought Molnija up short. "Anyway. Think it over. *Auf Wiedersehen.*"

The captain wheeled Molnija around and then galloped swiftly away.

Max watched them go as far as the horizon with eyes that were full of contempt.

"'Lightning,' he says. Did you hear him, Taras? What would you say if I gave you a new German name after all these years?"

Taras barked and put back his ears and growled as if the idea appalled him, too.

Max spat and looked up at the leaden sky, which was full of snow, although he could have wished for a real bolt of lightning to strike down the SS captain or, at the very least, to knock him off his horse.

THAT NIGHT, THERE WAS a blizzard that turned the sky the same color as the ground. It seemed that everything outside was white.

Inside his cottage, Max built up the fire, threw an old horse blanket in front of the gap under his front door, filled a ceramic hot-water bottle to cradle on his lap as he sat in his armchair, swaddled himself with fur rugs and thought himself very fortunate that he wasn't abroad on the steppe, for, in the depths of a Ukrainian winter, there is no enemy as bitter and determined as the northeasterly wind. It rattled the door, leaned against the window and penetrated the smallest cracks in the walls and the floorboards. That something as usually tranquil as air could behave with such violence never ceased to astonish Max.

"Even a snowman might feel inclined to come inside

on a night like this," he told Taras, and blew on the ember in the bowl of his pipe only for the comfort of seeing it glow. "Just to catch his breath and warm his toes."

Max was thinking he would have to go to bed to get properly warm when the dog lifted his head off the threadbare Persian carpet—a gift from the baron—growled and then walked to the door.

"What is it, Taras?" asked Max. "Can't be one of them Germans. They wouldn't have come all the way out here on a night like this. Even if they and their consciences did want me at their blessed horse-meat supper."

Taras barked once and then backed away from the door.

"A wolf, do you think?" He put down his pipe.

Taras stayed silent.

"Not a wolf, then," said Max, but he fetched his rifle all the same before he kicked the horse blanket away from the door and opened it. Taras advanced bravely onto the porch and barked once again.

Max peered into the snow-charged darkness with his gun in his hands.

"Who's there?" he asked, first in Ukrainian, then in Russian and once more in German. "Speak up. I'm in no mood for practical jokes."

There was no answer, but from the dog's behavior, he knew something was out there, so he brought one of the storm lamps and raised it at arm's length in front of him. The cyclone of blown snow dropped for a moment, as if stilled by the light, and what the old man saw as the vortex cleared left him breathless and amazed.

It was a girl, about fourteen or fifteen years old, tall, strong-limbed but very thin, with long, dirty brown hair, and as fearful as a rabbit in a trap. On a night such as this, any visitor—especially a young girl—would have been remarkable, but even more remarkable was the fact that she was accompanied by two Przewalski's horses, one on each side, so that they shielded the girl with their thick bodies from the worst of the northeast wind. And not just any of the Przewalski's horses—for although they were covered with snow, Max recognized the lead stallion Temüjin and his best mare, Börte, immediately.

"What's this?" the old man breathed, as if he were witnessing a miracle. "I must be seeing things. I don't believe it."

The girl was frightened of the ugly old man, but she was also desperate for his help.

"Please, sir," she said timidly. "My name is Kalinka. One of these horses is injured and needs your help." She pointed at the bloody flank of the mare. "Around these parts, they say no one knows more about the wild tarpan horses than you do."

"That's true, child," said Max, coming down the steps. "No one does. Not that it did the horses any good, mind, since I wasn't able to protect them from those blasted Germans. They've shot most of them. I wouldn't be surprised if these two are the last."

44

To his amazement, Börte stood still and allowed him near her. He bent over beside the mare and let the lamplight illuminate a wound in her shoulder.

"How do you get a name like Kalinka?" he asked the girl gruffly. "It's the title of a song, not someone's name."

"My real name is Kalyna," said the girl. "But my father used to call me Kalinka, and after a while, so did everyone else."

Max grunted. He didn't know much about girls, and what they were called or wanted to be called was of no real interest to him.

"There's something hard just under the mare's skin," he said, touching it gently. Again he marveled that the mare was prepared to tolerate his touch. "I could probably dig it out and patch her up if she'll let me. But that's the question. Will she let me? And here's another: where might you have come from on a night like this?"

"The woods up by the big lake," she said. "I've been living there since the late summer."

"It isn't summer now, child," said Max. "You'll die if you try and see winter out in this part of the world." He stood up. "I would suggest that you take them both around to the stable at the back of the cottage so that I can fix her up, but I never yet knew one of these horses who'd go where you wanted them to go."

"They'll go with me, I think," said the girl. "At least, they have until now."

Max handed her the lamp. Much to his surprise, the

45

two horses meekly followed the girl around the back of the cottage like a pair of lapdogs.

"Well, I never," he said to Taras. "It looks as if I don't know these horses half as well as I thought I did."

Max went inside, where he lit another oil lamp and fetched a black bag of surgical instruments and a bottle of disinfectant that one of the visiting Soviet state vets had left behind when everyone had fled from the Germans. He also brought a warm blanket for the girl and a piece of chocolate that the Germans had given him, which he'd been saving for a special occasion.

In the stables, he hung up the lamp and handed the girl the blanket and the chocolate.

"Here," he said. "Kalinka, is it? Your name?"

The girl nodded, wrapped herself in the blanket and started to eat the chocolate hungrily.

"Strikes me that the mare is not the only thing around here that needs looking after," said Max. "Where are your mom and dad, girl?"

"Dead." Kalinka uttered the word bluntly, without expression, as if she didn't even want to think about her mama and papa.

Max broke the ice in the water trough and brought some water in a pail to the horse's side. "Is there no one else to look after you? Grandparents? An aunt or an uncle?"

"They're all dead, too." Kalinka spoke quietly and calmly about this. She had learned you couldn't run when you were crying, and you couldn't stay silent inside a closet if you were weeping. When you couldn't trust anyone, you had to be able to rely on yourself. She had thought there would come a time for tears, but ever since her escape, this had not happened. She had now concluded that she might never cry again, that something human inside her had died alongside the rest of her family. "Three uncles, three aunts, my brothers, my sisters, my grandparents, my great-grandmother and all my cousins. Everyone had to gather in the botanical gardens in our city. Which is where it happened. I mean, where they and all the others were killed. Not just my family. But every family. At least every family that was Jewish. Fifteen or twenty thousand people. I'm not sure." She paused and then added: "As we were being marched to the botanical gardens, along Haharina Avenue, a door on the street opened for a moment, and someone just pulled me through and then closed it behind me again. It was a woman I'd never seen before. A woman who wasn't a Jew. It all happened in a few seconds. She took me to the back door of her building and told me to run away as quickly as possible and not to turn back, no matter what I heard. That my survival depended on running away. So I did. I ran away. And I've been running ever since."

For a moment, Kalinka remembered the sound of the shots and the screams she had heard as she ran away, and she shuddered, for she felt ashamed that she was alive and everyone in her family was not. How could she have done such a thing? This was the thought that haunted her, day and night.

Max was silent as he considered what Kalinka had just told him. "I thought it must have been something like that," he said.

"Before I escaped, I asked my grandfather why they were picking on the Jews," said Kalinka. "And he said that being a chosen people is a coin with two sides. Sometimes it's heads, he said, but just as often it's tails. He was making a joke, I think. My grandpa was like that. Always making jokes."

Max nodded. "I understand."

"By the way," she said, abruptly changing the subject, "thanks for the chocolate. I'd forgotten how good it tastes."

Max started to wash the mare's wound. Again, the horse didn't shy away when he touched it.

"And where was this, then? Your home city. You're not from round these parts, I reckon."

"It's not my home. Not anymore. I don't have a home. I mean, you can't, can you? Not without a family. It's family that makes a home, don't you think?"

Max shrugged. It had been a long time since he had thought about home in the way that she was describing, but all the same he knew she was right; unless there's someone or something to care for, the whole idea of home is meaningless. It was fortunate that he remembered Taras, his dog, whom Max cared for a great deal and who he thought must care for him almost as much.

"All right, I understand that. But where was this? I'd still like to know, Kalinka."

"Dnepropetrovsk."

"Dnepropetrovsk? Why, that's almost three hundred and fifty kilometers north of here!" said Max.

"Is that all?" said Kalinka. "It felt like more."

"Good grief, you mean to tell me that you've walked all this way? Alone?"

"Walking is easy when you've no place to go."

"Aye, there's a truth, right enough."

"But a geography lesson, I don't need. Please, look to the mare, will you? I don't want to talk about this anymore. There's no point in it, you see. What good would it do? It certainly won't bring any of them back, will it?"

All of her timidity was gone now; Max put the change in her down to the chocolate.

"No, I suppose not."

Having washed and disinfected the wound, Max did the same with his forceps. At the same time, he was carefully watching Temüjin, the stallion, who was watching him. The horse met his eye with an attentive intelligence he found slightly unnerving.

"There's a bullet in Börte's shoulder," said Max. "Just under the skin. It was more or less spent when it hit her, which explains why it's not any deeper in the flesh, but it's still going to hurt when I dig it out." It felt like

49

he was explaining himself to the stallion as much as to the girl.

"My father used to say that if you can't endure the bad, then you won't live to see the good," said Kalinka.

Max let that one go; it seemed rude to point out to the girl the obvious irony in her father's words. But she was there ahead of him.

"Not that he did, of course," she muttered. "Live to see the good, I mean." She shrugged. "But that doesn't stop it from being true, though."

"No, it doesn't."

Even now Max hesitated to probe Börte's wound for the bullet.

"Go on," said Kalinka. "What are you waiting for? She can take the pain. These tarpan horses are tough." Max glanced at Kalinka and considered that, given all she had been through, the girl might just be as tough as the horse.

"That's true," he said. "But what's also true is that I've had too many bites and kicks from these horses not to be in a hurry to get more of the same." He frowned. "Strictly speaking, they're not tarpans at all. I know that's what the locals call them. Tarpan, or *takhi*. But they're actually Przewalski's horses."

"It's a vet she needs, not a zoologist."

"Yes. All right. You're very impatient, aren't you?"

"Do you want me to hold her head?" asked Kalinka, ignoring his zoologist's explanation.

"I should like to see you try," said Max.

Kalinka shrugged and put her arms around the mare's

50

neck. "Hey," she told the mare. "It's going to hurt for a moment, but then it will be all right." She caught Max's eye. "Go on. She's as ready as she'll ever be."

"You live long enough, you see everything," said Max, and pushed his forceps into the hole in the horse's shoulder.

Temüjin snorted and turned away as if he couldn't bear to look and drank some of the water in the trough. In truth, he was rather squeamish for a wild horse and didn't care for the sight of blood at all.

Börte lifted one hoof and began to pace at the floor; if Max hadn't known better, he might have said that Börte was counting through her pain—almost as if she was trying to distract herself from what was happening with the forceps.

Finally, Max lifted the forceps nearer the light to reveal a piece of metal smeared with the mare's blood. He showed it to Kalinka, who simply nodded.

He disinfected the wound again and inspected it. "That's all done."

"Aren't you going to put anything on that?" asked Kalinka. "Stitch it, maybe? That's what my mama would have done."

"These horses heal better the natural way. Now that the bullet is out, she'll mend soon enough, I reckon. As long as we keep the wound clean, it should be all right. It's not likely she'll be rolling in any dirt for a while. With God's help, she'll be fine, I think."

"God," said Kalinka, and made a snorting noise that

51

had the stallion turning around to look at her curiously. "If he lived on earth, I think people would smash his windows. I know I would."

"I bet that's not something your grandfather said," said Max, washing his hands in the freezing pail of water.

Kalinka shivered under her blanket and did not reply.

"There's no point in trying to understand God," said Max. "If we did, he wouldn't be God, I think."

Max fetched the two horses some rice and some oats in a couple of pails from a big bag in the loft and watched them eat for a moment, simply taking pleasure that there was a pair of the horses that had escaped Captain Grenzmann and his men. With a pair, you could breed again.

"Any more of them alive, do you think?" he asked.

"I don't know," she answered. "The Germans killed almost all of them, I think. They're good at that."

"True," said Max. "Look, you'd better come into the cottage and get warm."

"What about the horses?"

"They'll be all right in here," he said. "I don't think anyone will come out here on a night like this. All the same, we'll move them somewhere safer in the morning. I'll leave them the light so they can finish their oats in comfort, although I suspect their vision is pretty good in the dark."

The sound of horses feeding greedily filled the stable.

"They are hungry, aren't they?" said Kalinka.

He smiled. "You look as though you could use some feeding yourself, Kalinka."

"I'm all right," she said.

But then she fainted, and it was clear to Max she wasn't all right at all. He scooped her up in his strong arms and carried her into the little blue cottage.

KALINKA HAD FAINTED BECAUSE she was starving; the four squares of dark chocolate given to her by the old man had reminded her of just how hungry she was. It had been three days since she'd last eaten something. But in front of his roaring log fire, swaddled in blankets, and with the old man's wolfhound lying on her feet, she quickly regained consciousness and drank a glass of hot sweet Russian tea from the samovar Max always kept lit when he was at home, and ate a piece of black bread and butter.

"Feeling better?" he asked her.

"Yes, thank you."

"Please don't mention it. I haven't much in the way of company these days, so you'll have to excuse my house-keeping. Sometimes, there's a German SS officer who stops by to water his horse in my stable and to give him some oats and rice—that's why there's a bag of feed in there—but he wouldn't ever dream of coming in here. Which is just as well. The Germans make me nervous." He shrugged. "Well, I suppose they make everyone nervous. For all the reasons you mentioned earlier."

Kalinka nodded, thinking she understood what the old man was too ashamed to come right out and say to her face.

"It's all right. I'll be on my way in just a minute, just as soon as I've finished this lovely tea. I wouldn't like to get you in any trouble."

"What are you talking about?" said Max. "You can't go anywhere on a night like this. You'd die of exposure."

"You really mean it? I can stay the night? Here? With you?"

"Stay the night and as long as you want, my girl. You're very welcome here."

"But I thought—what I mean is—well, everyone else I've been to for help since I left Dnepropetrovsk has told me to go away. And not as politely as that. They all said it was too dangerous for me to stay and drove me off with stones. Even when I was just sleeping in their barns or in their hayricks. Some of the local villagers set their dogs on me. Fortunately, I've always been good with dogs, so they didn't bite me."

She leaned down and patted Taras, who turned and licked Kalinka's hand as if he recognized someone who needed to feel some affection.

"You mean the villagers around here?"

Kalinka nodded. Before the old man had given her the chocolate, it had been months—perhaps longer—since anyone had shown her kindness.

Max sighed and shook his head. "It's true. And I know to my own cost that when people are afraid, they can be very cruel."

"The Germans bring that out in people," she said. "You are taking a risk, having me here; you know that, don't you? It might cost you very dearly."

"You let me be the judge of that, Kalinka." Max shrugged as best as he was able, with his neck the way it was. "Besides, if charity cost nothing, the world would be full of philanthropists." He poured her some more tea—only this time, he put an extra teaspoonful of jam in it.

"That's what my grandfather used to say, too."

"I like the sound of him," said Max.

Kalinka was quiet for a moment, and Max could see that he'd upset her by the mention of her grandfather again, so he quickly changed the subject.

"Look here, it seems obvious to me that you should live here at Askaniya-Nova," said Max. "For as long as you want. My wife disappeared or ran away a long time ago—I'm never quite certain which—and we never had a daughter of our own, although she should have liked one. Since you no longer have a father, or even a grandfather, it seems to me you're quite free to choose a replacement. I know I'm not much to look at, Kalinka. But looks aren't everything, they say. I should be more than honored if you were to live with me. For a spell, at least. Until you decide what you want to do."

Kalinka looked around the little cottage and thought for a moment. "But is it safe? I thought you said there was a German officer who stopped by here to water his horse sometimes. I doubt he's going to believe it if you tell him your niece has turned up to live with you. I have no papers. Suppose he asks for them. He'd be suspicious."

"That's true. Actually, I was thinking that I could hide you in an old waterworks nearby that was built by the old baron—he's the man who used to own the land around here—years ago, long before you were born. You and the horses, come to think of it. We'll have to hide them as well, won't we? That is, if they'll stay put. You, I think, we can trust to lie low, but about them, I'm not so sure. They're wild animals, after all, and don't like being in an enclosed space. I'm not at all sure those two—Temüjin and Börte—will still be in that stable in the morning."

"They'll stay. I'm sure of it."

"You seem to have made friends with them very quickly," said Max. "All my life I've known these horses. And they never followed me anywhere. What's your secret?"

"No secret," said Kalinka. "I suppose they trust me the way I guess I trust you. By instinct. And because we had something in common, I imagine. After all, we were all three of us hiding from the Germans."

Max nodded and smiled as Kalinka finished her hot, sweet tea noisily.

"This is good," she said.

"Have some more."

"I won't say no." As Max refilled her glass from the samovar and sweetened it with more jam, she asked him to tell her about the waterworks.

Max shook his head. "At one time, I contemplated living there instead of here myself. The place is large and quite dry, and it's nearby. I'll take you all there in the morning. No need to decide until then. Ask about your neighbors and then buy the house. That's what I always say."

"By the way," she asked. "Why do you call those horses Temüjin and Börte?"

"Ah. Good question. Well, it's simple, really. Temüjin has always been the dominant stallion among the Przewalski's horses, which more recently hail from Mongolia. Genghis Khan was a famous Mongol chief whose birth name was Temüjin, and Börte was his queen. And suddenly that name seems much more appropriate than I ever supposed it would be."

"Oh? Why is that?"

"Before Temüjin became the great Genghis Khan, he was hunted by a neighboring hostile tribe and forced into hiding. Here, have some more bread and butter. Poor child, you must be ravenous after all the walking you've done. Three hundred and fifty kilometers? It doesn't bear thinking of. I'm quite sure Moses himself couldn't have walked as far."

Max threw some logs on the fire and boiled a kettle for the hot-water bottle.

"Tell me, Kalinka. When did you last sleep in a bed?"

"Probably it was September." She shrugged. "There was a department store on Karl Marx Street where, during the day, I hid in a closet for several weeks; at night, I slept on a bed on the shop floor, before the cleaners found me and raised the alarm. But it's not so bad sleeping outside in summer and autumn."

"Well, tonight, you can have my bed. I'll have the chair."

"I couldn't take your own bed. No, that wouldn't be right."

"Do I look like one of the three bears? Really, I don't mind. Anyway, an old man like me doesn't sleep like he used to. So it's no great hardship. Just as often I fall asleep in the chair and that's good enough for me. What do I need with a bed?"

Max fetched her some more bread and butter, and for a moment, Kalinka just stared at them gravely.

"I'd forgotten," she said quietly. She had no words for how she felt anymore. Kalinka's feelings were buried so deep inside her, she could hardly remember where she'd put them. She could have no more smiled than she could have wept.

Max knelt down beside her and took her softer, smaller

hand in his great, gnarled paw and rubbed some more warmth into it.

"Here, here," he said. "Cheer up. You're quite safe now, I can assure you. Now tell me, little Kalinka, what it is that you think you've forgotten."

"Until just now I'd forgotten what it is to have someone be nice to me."

Max grunted modestly.

"So," said Kalinka. "I've told you my story. I think you should tell me yours."

"What makes you think I have one?"

"Because yours is an interesting face. As my father used to say, 'I don't think you got a face like that singing in a choir.' At the very least, I should like to know the name of the person who is looking after me."

"Fair enough," said the old man. "My name is Maxim Borisovich Melnik."

"And your story?"

"What story would that be, then?"

"The story of your life, perhaps?"

The old man hesitated. "No one was ever interested in hearing about my life before," he admitted.

"Well, I am, Maxim Borisovich Melnik." Kalinka glanced at the window.

"Unless you count the secret police."

"You see?" said Kalinka. "I knew you had an interesting face. Besides, it's a perfect night for a story, don't you think?"

Max nodded. "That it is," he admitted. "And I daresay mine will do the job right enough if it's a story for going to sleep that you're after."

"It isn't," said Kalinka. "Tell me about yourself. How did you come here? And when? And why? Please, Max. It's been a long time since anyone told me a story at bedtime."

MAX LIT HIS PIPE and looked into the distance for a moment as he tried to recollect the details of his life and how he first came to work for the baron.

"The reserve at Askaniya-Nova owes its existence to a German," said Max.

Kalinka pulled a face. "If it has Germans in it, I don't think I'm going to like your story," she said.

"Believe me, not all Germans are like the SS," said Max. "Even today, I'm sure that back in Germany, there are good Germans. The baron—the baron Friedrich Falz-Fein—was just such a German, for he was a wonderful man. It was he who created this place back in 1889. In its day, this was the largest private zoo in Europe, with over two hundred species of birds and more than fifty species of animals with hooves, such as bison, camels, deer, antelope, llamas and zebras. And, as well as a wide variety of birds that commonly make their home in this part of the world, there are cranes and pelicans from Africa and even a few ostriches. You should see the eggs they lay for breakfast. Enormous!" Max laughed, then continued.

"I was just twenty when I came to Askaniya-Nova from my hometown of Sevastopol, in 1897, as a groom for Baron Falz-Fein's Hanoverian horses, a breed that is one of the finest in the world. But it was 1902 before the first Przewalski's horses joined us here, and 1904 before a stallion arrived—a gift from Tsar Nicholas the Second—enabling the baron to begin a breeding program on his nature reserve, where the conditions for Przewalski's are more or less ideal. And together he and I oversaw a substantial increase in the number of Przewalski's horses, which is to say the numbers of these horses at Askaniya-Nova more than doubled in less than ten years.

"Even today, it's for the Przewalski's horses that the nature reserve is best known. These prehistoric horses are thought to have diverged from the modern horse about a hundred and sixty thousand years ago. Easily recognizable on ancient cave paintings found all over Europe and Asia, the Przewalski's horse is the rarest horse in the world. Until an explorer saw the horse in 1881 on a trip to central Asia, it was thought to be as extinct as the dodo."

"That's a bird, isn't it? From the island of Mauritius."

"Aye, that's right. Sailors killed them all for food. They

reckon the last dodo was seen in 1681. Curious-looking creature. Can't say I think much of it. It's no wonder you don't see any cave paintings of dodos, in my opinion."

The old man puffed his pipe for a moment, which seemed to stimulate a memory of something. "Here," he said. "I've got some pictures of those cave paintings. If I can find those books the baron gave me."

He began to search the cottage, and while he was opening a cupboard, some old newspapers fell on his head.

"Well, don't stop telling me your story," insisted Kalinka. "You can keep telling it while you look for them, can't you, Max?"

"Yes," said the old man, brushing the dust off himself. "I daresay you're right. Well, where was I?"

"You were saying how you and the baron doubled the number of Przewalski's horses in ten years."

"So I was. This is where my story gets interesting, I suppose. That's another way of saying that life has a funny habit of playing tricks on anyone who happens to be enjoying it, as I was. The same way I daresay lots of people were enjoying their lives in this part of the world. Fifty years of history has been very hard on Ukraine. And on the poor Falz-Feins, as you'll hear.

"Following the Bolshevik Revolution of 1917, the Communists confiscated Askaniya-Nova from the Falz-Fein family. Luckily for him, he was back in Germany when the revolution happened. But his aged mother, the baroness Sofia-Louise, wasn't so fortunate. She was living in her house in the nearby port of Khorly. The Bolsheviks— that's what people used to call the Communists—they ordered her to leave Ukraine and return to her native Germany. But she was a stubborn old girl and she refused. She also refused to surrender her estates, including Askaniya-Nova, and for this act of resistance, that brave old lady was shot by Communist guardsmen."

"How awful," said Kalinka.

"Yes, it was. But the Communists weren't finished. Like I said, I'm from Sevastopol, in the Crimea. So I'm not German myself, but I had learned the German language from the baron and the old lady, and when the Communists took over the reserve—this must have been 1919—they suspected me of being a German spy. I was arrested by the NKVD—the Communist secret police— who put me in prison and tortured me."

"And I thought it was just the Germans who could treat people so horribly," said Kalinka.

"Would that were true," said Max. He was looking under the bed for the books now. "But what happened to me was nothing. A terrible famine in Ukraine, deliberately caused by the Communists about ten years ago, resulted in the deaths of at least fourteen million people."

"How could they do something like that deliberately?" asked Kalinka.

"Because the leader of the Communists is a terrible man called Stalin, who decided that all of the food produced by the people of Ukraine should be fed to workers in factories in order to produce steel for tanks and guns. He thought steel was more important than people, see? Which ought not to be a surprise to anyone, given that's what his name means. *Stalin:* 'man of steel.' Anyway, I may have been tortured, but at least I'm still alive, which is more than those poor folk can say."

"So they let you go eventually?" asked Kalinka.

"Yes. After some months, the NKVD decided I wasn't a spy after all and I was cleared of all charges. Meanwhile, Askaniya-Nova was taken into state ownership and declared a People's Sanctuary Park in 1921, and so I returned to live here and look after the animals. Matter of fact, I think that's why they dropped the spying charges—so that I could come back here and be of some use to them. But I didn't mind. I love this place. I love the animals." Max laughed a hollow laugh. "I'd work here for nothing, which is just as well, as that's more or less what they paid me.

"At first, we did all right. At least with the breeding program. The Communists didn't really care about the reserve that much, but the horses were a different story; being as rare as they are, they're also worth a lot of money, and what the Communists wanted was to breed them so we could sell them to foreign zoos all over the world for hard currency. Which we did. Berlin, Warsaw, London. Just to give you some idea of how rare they are, Kalinka, before the Germans invaded in June 1941, there were just thirty-one Przewalski's horses living at Askaniya-Nova, which accounted for as much as half of the world's entire population of Przewalski's."

Finally, Max found the books he was looking for under a chessboard and a pile of old blankets.

"Aha," he cried. "Here they are."

Max brought the books over to Kalinka and laid one of them on her lap, where he opened it carefully and showed her some color pictures of ancient horses that were painted on the walls of caves.

"These pictures were taken in caves at a place called Font-de-Gaume, in France," said Max, "where there are paintings of more than forty prehistoric horses. It is plain to see why zoologists all over the world were so excited by the rediscovery of the Przewalski's horses, for they are identical to the horses in the paintings made by French cavemen more than seventeen thousand years ago."

"But why," asked Kalinka, "are they called Przewalski's horses?"

"That was the name of the man who rediscovered them, of course. Nikolai Przewalski was a Russian explorer."

"I see." Kalinka nodded. "Yes, I can see why people like your baron got so excited. The horses on the reserve—they're exactly like the ones in these cave paintings."

"They're a living fossil, is what they are," explained Max. "It was like finding a Neanderthal man or a saber-toothed tiger. You see, little Kalinka, there's so much in our world that changes very quickly. Quicker than seems comfortable, sometimes. But whenever I see a Przewalski's horse, I think of one of these cave paintings and I know I'm seeing exactly what our ancient forebears saw." He shrugged. "I like the way that makes me feel small. Like I don't matter very much in the scheme of things. I suppose that's why I'm so fond of these little cave horses."

He shook his head.

"Not that I always was," he admitted. "At first, I cared not a bit for them. For one thing, they kick and bite like the very devil. And I suppose I much preferred the more obvious breeding and beauty of the big Hanoverian horses that enjoyed lives of enormous privilege and comfort—better than many peasants—in the baron Falz-Fein's well-appointed stables. A bit like the baron himself, if the truth be told. But as I listened to and learned from the baron—who had read every book and paper about the wild horses, ever since Colonel Przewalski had rediscovered them—I found myself becoming as enthusiastic about the cave horses as he was."

Kalinka tried and failed to restrain a yawn. She felt warm and comfortable and, above all, safe for the first time in many months—certainly since she had run away from Dnepropetrovsk. The old man's voice was so soothing and friendly that it was hard to keep her eyes open. He might have looked frightening—there was something wrong with his neck that stopped him from turning his head properly—but there was no doubting his kindness.

"You're tired," said Max. "You need to sleep for a hundred years, like Sleeping Beauty, and get your strength back."

He picked her up like she weighed no more than a feather and carried her over to the bed, where he covered her with a thick fur rug. Instinctively, Taras climbed up onto the bed beside the girl, licked her face and then snuggled up close to her in order to help with the important business of keeping their guest warm.

"But why did the horses become extinct at all?" asked Kalinka, wiping her cheek with her sleeve. "They seem much too clever to be so easily wiped out. And why are the SS shooting them now?"

Max relit his pipe, drew up a chair by the bed and sat down.

"Over the years, I've come to the conclusion that it was their cleverness that was their undoing," he said. "Because they were almost impossible to catch and domesticate like other horses, it was simply easier for ancient tribesmen to kill and eat them—especially since the horses competed with cattle for what was sometimes rare and valuable grazing. And driven away in small scattered herds all over Asia, the horses decreased drastically in number, to the point of extinction that we see now."

He shrugged. "The Nazis," he said, "now, they're a very different story. They think that anything that's not German is second-rate. German people are superior and so are German horses. Anything else is to be enslaved or exterminated."

He was going to tell her exactly what Captain Grenzmann had told him about the Przewalski's but stopped himself as Kalinka was already asleep.

"Poor child," said Max. "I reckon she's had a pretty rough time of it, Taras. How did she ever walk all the way from Dnepropetrovsk?"

Taras whined with sympathy and laid his long wolfhound's muzzle across the girl's stomach.

"You feel sorry for her, too, eh?" The old man grinned. "I knew someone had been stealing bread and cheese when I was out of the house. And I was right. It must have been her. No question about it."

Taras sighed.

"It's all right, all right. Don't concern yourself, old dog—I'm not about to throw her out for stealing a bit of bread and cheese. It's obvious she was starving. I meant what I said, you know. She can stay here as long as she wants. Well, not in here. It's not so safe with that captain around when he feels like it. But I reckon she'd be safe enough at the old waterworks. What do you reckon?"

Taras jerked his long tail and moved closer to the girl as, outside the little blue cottage, the wind moaned like a wandering spirit.

THE NEXT MORNING, MAX awoke at his usual early time; it was a bitterly cold morning but at least it had stopped snowing. Instead of waking Kalinka, he went to the little stable at the back of the cottage to see if the two Przewalski's horses were still there and found—to his considerable surprise—that they were.

"There's nothing that makes another day feel quite as new as something you've never seen before," he said.

The stallion, Temüjin, looked up from the hay he was eating and gave the old man a look of near contempt, as if to say, "Your trouble is that you have no faith; she said we'd be here and we're here." In spite of this, Max still adopted a degree of caution when inspecting Börte's wound, for Przewalski's stallions are jealous of anyone looking at their mares, even humans.

"Now don't kick me," he told the stallion, "for my shins

and my backside are too old to learn a lesson I thought I already knew by heart."

Max was pleased to see that the wound showed no sign of infection, but all the same he cleaned and disinfected it again, just to be on the safe side. Then he fed the horses some more oats mixed with rice and went back to the cottage to wake Kalinka with some breakfast. He brought her a little inlaid wooden tray with hot porridge, sweet Russian tea and some black bread and a piece of honeycomb.

"I must be dreaming," she said sleepily.

"No, it's not a dream," he said. "You're here, all right. And I'm glad of the company. Which is not something I've said in a long time."

Kalinka glanced at the black window with her one open eye. "It feels like it's still the middle of the night."

"Aye, it's still dark, right enough," admitted the old man. "But I want to move you and the horses to the waterworks before it gets light, in case that German captain appears on his morning ride. He doesn't often come this way. But he might. Just out of pique. On account of how I didn't go and have dinner in the mess with his men the other night."

"A free meal? Why didn't you?"

Max shrugged. "I had my reasons. And it's just as well I stayed here; otherwise I might have missed meeting you and the horses."

"Who would have been out on a night like that?" said Kalinka.

"Suppose I'd been like those villagers and turned you away?"

Kalinka ate a spoonful of thick porridge, pulled a face and shook her head. "No. That wasn't a possibility."

"Why not?"

"Because of the horses. Maybe I didn't explain things properly. It was them that brought me to your door. It was the horses that were rescuing me, just as much as I was rescuing them. I suppose they knew I couldn't have survived another night in the woods. Not in that blizzard. They knew you weren't going to turn me away; otherwise they wouldn't have brought me here. In the same way, they knew that you could dig that bullet out of Börte's shoulder. At least that's the conclusion I've come to. I know these horses, and I think they just know things that you wouldn't expect horses to know."

"Yes, I've always thought that's true," admitted Max. "Yes, they're very smart. As you must be yourself, Kalinka, to have remained at liberty for so long."

She shrugged. "It's not so difficult to be on your own." She shrugged again. "Sometimes it's more difficult to be with people, you know?"

"That's true, right enough. There's nothing as queer as other people, I reckon."

"After I got out of Dnepropetrovsk, I was with the partisans for a while. In the forest. Resistance fighters. But they wanted me to wash and cook for them. Anyway, after they tasted my cooking, they gave me a gun and told me to come and fight with them. They said if I was

73

going to kill people, then it might as well be Germans. But I didn't want to kill people, even Germans. So one night I ran away."

"Sounds like you have plenty of horse sense of your own, child."

"Maybe. My father used to have several horses for his work. Big draft Vladimirs. There was one called Shlomo—I used to talk to him a lot. He was a very sensible horse."

"What kind of work did your father do?"

"He worked for the state fuel merchant, delivering wood and coal to people. He used to say that sometimes he thought the horses could have done the job themselves. They knew their routes the way I know my alphabet. But sensible as he was, Shlomo was a dunce next to the two outside. They might be a bit untidy-looking, but underneath their shaggy coats, they're as smart as a crow with a top hat and a fancy gold watch."

"You know, you're a little untidy yourself," observed Max. "I bet that underneath all that grime, there's a pretty girl. I shall have to find you a brush and a comb, a toothbrush and some clean clothes. You can wash when we're in the waterworks."

Max glanced nervously at the window. A bar of red had appeared on the horizon, indicating that dawn was just around the corner.

"Come on. We'd better get moving."

They went outside to the stable, where the Przewalski's were already waiting patiently by the door.

"See what I mean?" said Kalinka. "They just know what you're thinking."

But Max wasn't listening. His eyes were on the horizon. His neck might have been next to useless, but there was nothing wrong with his eyesight and he had already spied a dot that was moving rapidly toward them from the direction of the big house.

"What is it?" asked Kalinka.

"That SS captain—Grenzmann," said Max. "Up and around much earlier than usual and coming this way at a gallop. Come on, back inside the stable. Before he gets near enough to see you."

"Maybe that's why he's galloping," suggested Kalinka, herding the horses back into the stable.

"No. He gallops because he's a German. The Germans do everything at a gallop. Maybe if they stopped and took some time to think before they did something, they wouldn't be in the mess they're in now. And more importantly, neither would we."

"Perhaps I should just make a run for it. With the cave horses."

"No," said Max. "You wouldn't make it. The horse he rides isn't called Lightning for nothing. Besides, the captain carries a sidearm. And I don't think he's the type who'd hesitate to use it."

"It's all my fault," said Kalinka. "I should never have come here. I'm going to get you into trouble, aren't I?"

"You keep these two quiet, if you can," said Max. "And I'll try to get rid of him."

"Suppose he leads his horse in here for a drink or some feed?" asked Kalinka.

Max shook his head and tried to conceal the panic he was feeling. "Just do as I say and everything will be fine," he said. But he wasn't at all sure about that.

The old man went out of the stable, picked up his axe and began chopping wood while he waited for the captain to arrive at the cottage; he wondered if he might after all be capable of using the axe against the captain if Grenzmann threatened the girl and the horses.

Finally, the captain arrived and, as usual, he was full of smiles and impeccable good manners.

"Isn't it a wonderful morning, Max?" he said, breathing heavily.

Max looked up at the sky almost as if he hadn't noticed it before and nodded.

"You've brought the sun with you, sir," he said agreeably.

Captain Grenzmann turned in his saddle and looked behind him.

"Yes, you're right, Max, I think I have." He lit a cigarette and smoked it thoughtfully. "I wanted to see the steppe in the dawn while the snow was still perfect."

"I expect that's the artist in you, sir," said Max. "Not the soldier."

"Yes, you're right about that, too. Sometimes, I think I should like to come back and live here, after the war, and paint this wonderful place. The colors here are always changing, just like an artist's palette. I've never painted landscapes and I have an idea I'd be very good at it."

"I'm sure you would be, sir."

"I would have painted it before but I don't have any paints. Just my pen and my inks. And you can't do justice to a dawn like that with just pen and ink. Can you?"

"No, sir."

"You know, I'm a little disappointed in you, Max. I thought we were friends."

"It's kind of you to say so, sir."

"Well, yes, it is, under the circumstances. It's not every Russian peasant who gets asked to dinner by an SS battalion. We missed you last night, Max."

"I would have come but for the blizzard, sir."

"I wonder about that. I mean, I know you have a pocket watch, Max. And I noticed it didn't start snowing until well after eight o'clock, by which time we'd already begun to eat."

Max shrugged. "That's true. But I took one look at the sky and I just knew it was going to be bad. So I stayed home."

Grenzmann jumped down from the saddle and tossed the reins behind him.

"Well, then, it's lucky for you that I feel able to ask you again for tomorrow night."

"Tomorrow night?"

"Yes. I believe we're having goulash, made from horse meat, of course. But you won't know the difference, believe me. Last night, the cook made sauerbraten and I couldn't have told you if it was horse or beef he used. Really, I couldn't. So. Will you come?"

Had it not been for his concealed guests, Max would certainly have refused, but all he could think of now was how to get rid of the captain as quickly as possible.

"Yes, sir. And it's kind of you to ask me. Of course I'll come."

"Good."

Molnija lifted his nose in the air and snorted; then he clapped his hoof on the snow and lowered his head as if trying to find some grass. If Max hadn't known that the big Hanoverian stallion could smell the two Przewalski's horses, he might have said he was hungry.

"All that talk of food has made Lightning hungry, I think," said Captain Grenzmann.

Max threw down his axe. "If you'll wait here a moment, I'll bring him a bucket of feed, sir."

"Don't trouble yourself, Max," said Grenzmann. "We can help ourselves, can't we, boy?"

"It's no trouble at all," he said, hurrying toward the stable. But Molnija was already trotting there on his own ahead of him.

"Really, Max," said Grenzmann, striding after him. "I can do it. You're not my servant. Not when you're here, at your own home. As I said before, you and I are friends. I feel there's a bond between you and me. Perhaps it's because of the way you speak German, I don't know. It's strange. But there it is."

With Grenzmann close on his heels, Max hurried around the corner just in time to see Molnija turn into the stable. Surely, he thought, the game was up now; with any luck, Kalinka would have had the presence of mind to hide herself in the loft, but there was no way that Grenzmann was going to overlook the presence of two "forbidden" horses in Max's stable. He would very probably shoot the horses and then Max himself.

But when the old man reached the stable door, he found Molnija with his muzzle in a bucket of fresh feed— placed there, he imagined, by Kalinka—with no sign of Temüjin or Börte. Astonished, he glanced around the stable several times but, as if by magic, the two horses had vanished.

Grenzmann caught up with the old man and smiled. "I can see you were expecting us, Max."

"Sir?"

"The feed you had prepared. That was most thoughtful of you. A peace offering, perhaps?"

"Er, I did wonder if you might ride out this way, sir," said Max. "It being such a beautiful morning."

Grenzmann looked about him and took a deep breath.

"I wonder, how many more such mornings will there be for us Germans?"

"Many more, I hope, sir."

"What do you think will happen to Lightning when I leave, Max?"

"I haven't given it much thought, sir."

"Well, I have. Since that awful business with your

Przewalski's horses, it's been on my mind a lot. Shall I tell you what I think will happen to him? To Lightning? To all of your precious animals here at Askaniya-Nova?"

Max shrugged. He might have reminded the captain that almost all of the animals—the deer, the llamas, the bison, even the zebras—had been shot by the Germans for their kitchen, but he hardly wanted to provoke an argument with Grenzmann. Not when he was being so friendly.

"I think the Red Army will butcher this horse and then eat him. That's what will happen to him."

"Then why not take him with you, sir? When you leave."

"I'd like to, Max. Really, I would. But even a horse as fast as this couldn't keep up with a motorized group of SS. Especially as we may have to try to fight our way out of here."

Grenzmann let Molnija finish the last of the feed in the pail and then lifted his head into his hands.

"So what will you do, sir?"

"Only one thing I can do, really."

To the old man's relief, Grenzmann took hold of the horse's reins and then led him outside, where he mounted the animal again and turned him toward the big house.

"I shall shoot him myself." Grenzmann patted the horse on the neck and then smiled sadly at Max. "It's the kinder thing to do. That an animal as fine and noble as this should end up on some Russian peasant's plate is an unbearable thought to me."

Max said nothing.

"But that's not for a while yet." The captain nodded. "Don't forget about tomorrow night, will you, Max?"

"No, sir. I won't forget. And thank you."

Grenzmann galloped away, and for quite a while after he'd gone—until he realized it was the sound of his own heart beating—it seemed that Max could still hear the horse's hooves on the snow.

THE OLD MAN WATCHED Captain Grenzmann gallop away until he was just a dot on the snowy horizon before turning back to the stable. Still more than a little puzzled—for he had seen no tracks in the snow leading away from the stable to persuade him that Temüjin and Börte had ever left there—Max looked up at the loft and called out Kalinka's name.

"Kalinka," he said. "You can come down now. He's gone."

For a moment, Max thought there must be an earthquake—these are not uncommon in that part of the world—because the straw-covered floor of the stable seemed to shift before his eyes; the next second, Kalinka stood up, followed by the two horses.

"That was close," she said. "There was one moment when his stupid, great horse almost stepped on me."

"I don't believe it," said Max, for it was now apparent to him that all three of them had been hiding under a layer of straw.

She grinned. "We really fooled him, didn't we? That German. And his German horse."

"How did you do it?" he asked the girl.

"Believe me," she said, picking straw off her clothes, "I've hidden in a lot of hayricks since I left Dnepropetrovsk. More than I care to remember."

"I'm sure you have. But what I mean is, how on earth did you persuade these two horses to lie down and let you cover them with a layer of straw?"

"Actually, it was their idea," said Kalinka. "They lay down and started to pull the straw across themselves, like they were going to bed. I just helped finish the job. You know, I'd say they've done this sort of thing before: hiding. I mean, they seem pretty good at it. As good as me, I reckon. Maybe better."

"For years, I've been telling people that these horses are as clever as foxes."

"I reckon they are, you know. Not that I know many foxes."

"I used to say that there was a very good reason why they had a fur brush for a tail instead of just hair." Max rubbed his silver beard thoughtfully. "I guess I should have listened to myself, eh?"

He laughed, clapped his hands and stamped around the floor with delight. This prompted Temüjin to utter a

83

whinny and hoof the straw, which seemed to amount to almost the same thing.

"I always knew they could find the right spot to stand in that helped them blend in with a bush or a tree," added Max. "There are plenty of stories in the books about how they were able to evade Mongolian hunters who were just a few steps away from them. But I didn't realize how far they could take something like that. I never heard of a horse doing what I witnessed in here."

"There's a first time for everything," said Kalinka. "Isn't that what people say?"

"For everything except a miracle, perhaps." He shook his head. "Come on. I won't be happy until I've got the three of you hidden away again."

Max led them outside; the sun was properly up by now, and they could see a clear trail left by Grenzmann's horse as far as the horizon, which prompted Max to find something new to worry about.

"Oh, I hadn't thought of that," he said.

"What is it?"

He pointed at the Hanoverian horse's hoofprints.

"If we walk on this snow, there will be an obvious trail from here to the waterworks. For any German soldiers looking for more horses to shoot, it would be like drawing them a map."

"We could walk single file," suggested Kalinka. "Like Saint Wenceslas's page."

Max shook his head. "It would still make them curious. And that curiosity might lead them to the old water-works. No, I think it's probably best we keep its existence as secret as possible."

"So what are we going to do?"

He glanced up at the sky again. "There's only one thing we can do, I think, and that's to wait for it to snow again before we go to the waterworks."

"Is it going to snow again?"

"In this part of Ukraine, at this time of year, it always snows again," Max said grimly.

Kalinka shrugged and led the two horses back into the stable. "I suppose," she said, "we could always hide under the straw if that captain or any of his men come back."

Max nodded. "If my old heart can stand it, I suppose you could at that," he said.

"Until then we could play chess, if you like," said Kalinka. "I noticed that you have a set of pieces and a board."

"Do you play?"

"A little."

It was several hours before it started to snow again, by which time Kalinka had beaten the old man at chess three times in a row.

"You're very good at that game," he said irritably as he finally led the girl and the two horses across the open steppe to the smallest lake, which was where the water-works was located. "How is that?"

"My father said I was a prodigy," she announced matter-of-factly. "He could never beat me and he was

85

much better than you. Oh, I don't mean that you're no good at all. Just that you're not half as good as he was. He was the regional state chess champion. He used to say that the secret of being a very good player is to think two or three moves ahead. Somehow, I manage to think four or five moves ahead. That's all."

"That's all?" he muttered. "You manage to make that sound quite unremarkable, Kalinka."

"Do I?"

Max turned and looked back at their trail, which was already being covered by a light layer of snow; in an hour or two, the trail would have disappeared for good.

"But maybe that's how you've survived on your own for so long," he said. "By thinking four or five moves ahead."

"No," she said. "I think I've just been lucky. That's the difference between survival and chess. In chess, you don't need any luck at all."

"The way I play, you do."

"True." She paused for a moment and then added, "Being good at chess is a little like looking into the future. Mostly it's about seeing things that other people can't see."

Max shook his head. "Chess is one thing. But I think you've also seen things that people are never meant to see. Such as your mom and dad being killed. That's what makes you a survivor, Kalinka. That's what makes you so strong."

Kalinka didn't answer; she didn't feel particularly strong, but she felt that Max was probably right. Then again, it wasn't like she had much choice. Going on with her life was the only thing that she could do now—and not for herself but for her mama and her papa. Her own survival was something she had dedicated to them.

They reached the smallest lake, where the forest was at its thickest and most overgrown.

"The waterworks," he said. "It's in those trees."

Kalinka looked closely and then shook her head. "I can't see anything," she admitted.

"Good," said the old man. "That means the Germans won't see anything either."

He led the way through some thick undergrowth to a doorway in a brick-built structure not much taller than Kalinka that was almost invisible underneath the snow-covered vegetation. Max opened the door and then lit a lamp that was hanging on a hook on the wall inside.

"The baron built this place because it's difficult to provide a park of this size, surrounded by steppe, with enough water," he said, advancing along a low passageway. "Down there is the old pumping station. And out here—"

He opened another door to the outside and pointed to what looked to Kalinka like two circular stone huts.

"These are the old storage tanks. Water from these used to flow all over the reserve in pipes and canals that go underground. As you can see, we're completely surrounded with trees and bushes. The only way you could see these is if you were to fly over them. The tanks were both completely watertight until the earthquake of 1927. That put a big split in the wall of each of them and that was the end of the waterworks. Over the last ten years, the splits have got bigger, until now they're more like doorways. We'll put you in one tank and the horses in the other. But I reckon the horses can come and go and do their business out here within the perimeter of the trees without anyone noticing. Not even you, probably. There's an inspection window in the roof of each tank that should give you plenty of light in the day."

Kalinka stepped through the jagged doorway of the water tank and looked around. There was an old mattress, some boxes of junk and the makings of a fire.

"Has someone been living here?" she asked.

"Just me. Like I said, for a while, I considered living in here instead of the cottage. Gave it a shot for a couple of weeks one summer. You'll find some useful things in them boxes, I shouldn't wonder. Candles, lamps, some blankets, a few tins of food. It's quite cozy, actually. Light a fire under that window and the smoke will go up through the broken glass."

"What changed your mind? About living in here? I mean, there aren't any ghosts, are there?"

"Ghosts?" Max grinned. "Whatever gave you such an

idea? The only ghost around here is me. Since you ask, the reason I never stayed here was because it turns out I don't much like enclosed places. There's a name for it. Claustrophobia, they call it. So I stay in the cottage out on the steppe there, with all its faults. Besides, I like to see the birds on the lake in the spring. From my window, I have a fine view of all the ducks and geese that go swimming there. I especially like to watch the gray and purple herons that hunt for fish and frogs—from them, I think I've learned patience. It's like going to the cinema for me, I reckon." He frowned. "I know this place looks a bit grim now. But we'll soon get it looking a bit more homey. And you can have old Taras here for company. I'll bring some more stuff across from the cottage while it's still snowing."

"Don't worry," said Kalinka. "I've certainly stayed in many worse places since I left Dnepropetrovsk."

Kalinka thought of the cemetery in Nikopol where she had slept for almost a week: German bombs had opened up some of the crypts, and she had lived in one for several days before the grave diggers had come and chased her off. That had been one of the worst places, probably; she was sure there had been ghosts in that crypt. Tolerable during the day, but not a place to stay at night. It's hard to sleep in a cemetery because you always worry that you're never going to wake up.

"I expect you have, child. And I'm right sorry for it, so I am."

"Have you always lived here on your own, Max? I think you mentioned a wife."

The old man grimaced.

"Once, there was a girl I loved and married. Her name was Oxana Olenivna, and she worked as a maid for the dowager baroness Sofia-Louise, but she disappeared around the time that the old lady was murdered. I always supposed Oxana ran away or was sent to a labor camp by the secret police. Either way, it's been years since I've seen or heard of my wife, and I don't suppose that's ever going to change."

"And no one since her?" Kalinka asked. "No company at all?"

"Well, there's Taras here, but no, child. There have been no women since Oxana. Besides, what woman would look at me? The NKVD left my body looking so twisted and scarred that any normal woman would be repelled by a fellow like me."

"Was it them who hurt your neck?" asked Kalinka.

"It was. My neck was broken and mended badly so that my head sits stiffly on my shoulders—so stiffly that if I want to look around, I have to turn my whole body to do it. As you can see."

Kalinka bit her lip and, reaching out, touched his neck gently with her hand. "Does it hurt?" she asked.

"No, it doesn't hurt. Not now. To be honest, I've gotten used to the inconvenience of having a neck that is useless to me. Besides, I can do everything an able-bodied man can do—sometimes more, because pain means little to me now. There's no pain I ever encountered that could compete with the disappearance of my wife and the death of the baroness and the fact that the baron can never again return from Germany to Askaniya-Nova." He thought for a moment and then added: "And the murder of those horses, of course."

"I'm sorry," said Kalinka. "For all your trouble."

"Don't feel sorry for me, child. I'm a very fortunate fellow. I have plenty of wood for my fire, which has a bread oven made of stone. I've plenty to eat. In summer, I fish for lampreys, and I pick soft fruit from the bushes. Sometimes I go hunting for small game—squirrels and rabbits, mostly—but in truth, I hate killing anything. I could happily live without the meat, but as you've discovered, the fur is essential to survive the bitter cold of our Ukrainian winters.

"Not that I dislike winter, mind. I love its harsh simplicity, the thick blanket of snow that makes everything eerily quiet so that you can hear a pheasant a hundred meters away, the pure, cold air, and the excuse to build up a good fire and stay late in bed. But my favorite season is the early summer, when there are wild strawberries on the ground and plums on the trees, and the magnolia trees are covered with white flowers as if the branches were heavy with snow."

"I don't think I shall ever really enjoy a summer again," admitted Kalinka. "I think that I shall always remember that the Germans came to Dnepropetrovsk in the summer. And killed my family."

"I think you've had a very hard life for one so young," said Max. "But all things considered, it's a lot better than the alternative."

K ALINKA WRAPPED HERSELF IN blankets and furs, and stayed close by the fire that Max lit for her. There was plenty of dry wood stacked around the inside of the water tank, and they soon had the place feeling much warmer. The old man made several journeys to the cottage to bring food for Kalinka and the horses, an old samovar, a brush and comb, some oil lamps so she could look at the books with the pictures of the cave horses again, and the chessboard. Max even spent the night there in case she was scared.

Kalinka awoke in the night and fetched herself a drink of water. But when she saw the old man and Taras asleep by the fire, she found that she could not go back to sleep, at least not right away—not when she could just sit with her head on her knees and look at them both for a while and reflect on how nice it is to have someone looking out for you. To have someone who cares for you and thinks of you as a person, not only as a Jew or as an escaped prisoner or as someone to set your dog on. She realized that for the first time since Dnepropetrovsk, the knot in her stomach had all but disappeared; soon afterward, she fell asleep and dreamed of staying at Askaniya-Nova with Max and Taras forever.

The next day, Max let the girl sleep until well after dawn and managed to make a samovar of hot tea before she was awake.

Swaddled in furs, Kalinka sat up and leaned against the curved stone wall as he laid a little wooden tray on her lap and pointed out the good things that were there besides the hot black tea with a spoonful of strawberry jam in it.

"There's warm scones," he said, "butter and jam, some cheese-filled pierogies, a couple of hard-boiled eggs and some pickled gherkins."

"What service," she said. "You're spoiling me, Max."

"After all you've been through, I think you could do with a bit of spoiling, girl. Not to mention fattening up. I never saw anyone as thin as you. Except perhaps during the famine of 1932. Yes, there were lots of thin people around then."

"This is like the Astoria Hotel in Dnepropetrovsk," she said. "My father took us all there on my mother's fiftieth birthday. And it was such a beautiful place. We had afternoon tea with cakes in a little silver basket, like we were in a novel by Tolstoy, and then we went for a walk in Globy Park. It was the last time we were all together as a family. My elder brother, Pinhas, went to the army after that; he was killed in the Battle for Smolensk in July 1941, and the rest—well, I told you what happened."

After breakfast, Max fed the Przewalski's horses and inspected Börte's wound. Having declared that the mare was on the mend, he spent the rest of the morning and half the afternoon trying without success to beat Kalinka at chess.

"It's no good," he laughed. "You're too strong a player for me. I don't think I could beat you, child."

"You're out of practice," she said kindly.

"Practice, nothing," he roared in a good-humored sort of way. "You're too good for me, that's all."

"What do you normally do in the evenings around here?" she asked.

"What do you think I do?" he said, chuckling. "In winter, I smoke my pipe until it's dark and then go to bed. But in summer, when it's light until quite late, things are different. I sit outside on the veranda there and watch the sun paint the sky. He's quite an artist, is the sun, you know. I heard one of those Germans talking about the meaning of life, and I thought to myself, I don't know a better meaning than the contemplation of the universe and all of God's works."

Kalinka appreciated the simplicity of the old man's philosophy.

"Haven't you got a radio?" she asked. "Or a gramo-phone?"

"Now, what would I want with a radio?" he said. "From what I've heard on the radio, it's mostly just lies about how rosy everything is in the country. My wife had a gramophone, but I broke the only disc it had. Borodin's *Prince Igor*, I think it was."

Kalinka nodded. "Then I suppose we will have to play chess," she said.

"Not tonight, we won't," said Max. "I have to go to dinner with the Germans at the big house tonight. I don't want to go, especially since I know what's on the menu. But I don't have any choice now I've said I'll be there. They'll be offended if I don't turn up. And if there's one thing I've learned over the last two years, it's that it's best to avoid offending the Germans. Especially the SS." He grimaced. "Blast. I suppose I shall have to have a bath, too."

Kalinka frowned. "What *is* on the menu?"

"Horse meat," said Max. "It'll be the Przewalski's horses they slaughtered. I imagine they'll take a pecu-liarly sadistic delight in watching me try to eat it."

"I couldn't ever eat horse meat," said Kalinka, pulling a face. "Not if I live to be a hundred. I don't see how any-one who's lived and worked with horses could eat them. At least, that's the way I feel about it."

"Don't think I'm looking forward to it, because I'm not, but what could I do?" Max shook his head. "Under the circumstances, I couldn't very well refuse the captain's invitation. I was trying to get rid of him at the time, remember?"

Kalinka shrugged. "You might have got rid of him just as easily by turning down his invitation, don't you think?"

"Perhaps. Perhaps not. He says we're friends. And all I can say is that if he's a friend, then I'd hate to have an enemy. But, for the sake of the animals at Askaniya-Nova, I've always gone along with that idea, so as not to irritate him unnecessarily."

"Yes, I can see that's worked out well for them," said Kalinka. "Especially the horses."

Max shrugged unhappily. "It seemed the best thing to do at the time," he said. "But you could be right. After all is said and done, I haven't managed to achieve very much here, have I?" He smiled sadly and threw another log on the fire. "One way or other, I seem to have failed."

"I'm sorry," said Kalinka. "Dear Max, that was extremely rude of me. And you're wrong. You've achieved a great deal. Thanks to you risking your life, there are two Przewalski's horses still alive. Not to mention me."

"The horses are important, it's true," he said. "But I reckon you're what's important now. Keeping you alive is my priority."

Kalinka came over to the old man and hugged him fondly. "Do you forgive me? For being so unkind?"

"Of course, I forgive you, child."

Then she kissed his silver-bearded cheek, which made him grin. He touched his cheek with surprise and, for a moment, could not speak.

"It's been so long since anyone kissed me," he said, "I'd forgotten what it feels like."

Kalinka was so reminded of her own grandfather that she kissed him again.

"Here," he said, rubbing his cheek, "stop that, or I shan't be able to stop grinning and Captain Grenzmann shall think I've gone mad, or worse, start suspecting that I'm up to something. I've spent so long scowling at the Germans, they'll certainly think it very odd if I start to smile now."

"And you're right, of course," declared Kalinka. "You must go. Without question, staying on the right side of that SS captain is the best thing to do. If he thinks he's your friend, that's surely for the good; I should hate to imagine what he might be like if he decided you were his enemy. Although I must say I have a pretty shrewd idea."

"Yes, and so have I."

"It sounds as if you speak pretty good German. They taught us some German in school for a while. When our two countries were allies, that is. But I never liked the language very much."

"So there is something you're not very good at."

"No, I said I didn't like it. As a matter of fact, I learned to speak it quite well. That's another reason why I managed to escape from the botanical gardens. Later on, when

I was running away, I managed to convince an SS guard that I was German and that he had made a mistake."

"There's been a mistake, all right," said Max. "This whole war was a dreadful mistake. Many's the morning I wake and think it was all just a terrible dream. That I will walk outside and they'll be gone. If you could wish Germans gone, I'd have done it."

"One morning, you'll wake up and they will be gone. Didn't you say that they're losing the war?"

"Not quickly enough for my liking. The captain talks about fighting his way back to the German lines. But I just hope they don't decide to make a last stand here." He shook his head. "Well, I must get on. Like I said, I should have a bath. I'll come back tomorrow morning and bring you some more food. Then I'm going to search every kilometer of this reserve and see if I can't find some more of these horses. Maybe bring them back here for safety."

Max got up to leave and so did Taras.

"Stay here with Kalinka, Taras," said Max. "See that no harm comes to her."

Taras barked.

"Why is he called Taras?" asked Kalinka.

"I despair." Max frowned. "What are they teaching you in school these days? Taras is named after the hero of a book by a great Ukrainian writer called Nikolai Gogol—a Cossack named Taras Bulba."

"Sorry," said Kalinka. "But I never heard of it."

Max considered for a moment. "On second thought,

maybe that's not such a good book for you." He shrugged. "He's less than kind about Jews, is old Gogol. Anyway, he's a brave dog, aren't you, boy?"

Taras barked again.

"Pretty bright, too," said Kalinka. "Perhaps I'll teach him to play chess."

"Now, that's something I would like to see," said Max. He patted the dog's head, and then he patted Kalinka's head, and then he went away.

Kalinka went back to the fire and set out the chess set once more. She had been joking when she said she'd teach Taras how to play chess. All the same, Taras watched intently as she moved the pieces around. She hadn't played out positions on the board since she'd left Dnepropetrovsk, but just to have a chess set in front of her felt like a real luxury. Playing chess always calmed her and helped persuade her that, against all the evidence to the contrary, she was in control of her life.

After a while, it started to grow dark, so she lit one of the storm lamps, and with two apples from a wooden box that Max had given her, she went to see the Przewalski's horses in the other water tank. There was plenty of straw in there and they looked reasonably comfortable, but Kalinka still inquired after their welfare.

"How are you both?" she asked.

Temüjin flicked his furry tail and walked quickly around the perimeter of the tank as if he were in a circus ring.

"You don't like being inside. I know. But don't forget you can go outside. Just as long as you stay within the perimeter of trees."

Temüjin nodded patiently and snorted several times as if to say, "Yes, yes, I know, but it doesn't stop me wanting to run around the steppe at full speed in order to warm up."

"You'll have to be patient," said Kalinka. "It won't be long now until the Germans are gone, and then you both can run around the steppe as much as you want. Me too, I hope. I bet this place is wonderful in summer. I'm looking forward to seeing it."

Talking to the Przewalski's made her feel like she was in the stables at home again, before the war, when she'd spoken to her father's Vladimir horses every night before she went to bed. The Vladimirs had been three times the size of the Przewalski's, because it takes a big, heavy horse to haul a cartload of coal; they were also quieter and more patient, and this was just as well, she thought. A Vladimir that had behaved anything like a Przewalski's could have destroyed the city of Dnepropetrovsk in minutes. Not for nothing had armored knights once ridden these great horses into battle. And yet they were gentle giants: sometimes as a treat, her father had allowed Kalinka to sit on their backs and plait their long manes and tails with blue and white ribbons—which were the colors of Ukraine—that her mother gave her, and she still marveled that those animals could have been so patient and have allowed her to treat their manes like the hair on her doll.

There was nothing that she could have plaited into the manes and tails of the Przewalski's. Their manes stood up like the bristles on a toothbrush, while their strangely furry tails resembled *payos*—the long ringlets worn by some of her father's more devoutly religious friends. That was strange, but nothing to compare with the black-and-white stripes on the back of the legs of the horses, which reminded her of the stripes on a prayer shawl.

"I'm afraid there's no getting away from it," she told Börte as she stroked the mare's white face, "you're just different from other horses. Nothing wrong with that, of course. But I wonder: Can Max really be right about this? Could you really trace your ancestors back into prehistory?"

She opened the book that Max had brought over from the blue cottage. First she looked at the baron's bookplate on the inside front cover—a great coat of arms that looked like it belonged on a herald's flag; and then she found the color plates of the French caves.

"It says here that the paintings at Font-de-Gaume were discovered by a local schoolmaster in 1901," she told the two cave horses. "It's believed people first lived in the caves around 25,000 BC. There are forty horse depictions and twenty mammoth depictions. They're extinct, too. And that makes you two very special. Perhaps the two most special horses anywhere in the world right now."

Börte let out a snort that might have indicated modesty.

"You know," she told the cave horses, "I should love to see one of these cave paintings Max was talking about, for real. The ones that Paleolithic men painted."

Börte whinnied again.

She paused for a moment.

"What's that you say?"

Kalinka looked at the stone walls of the water tank and almost allowed herself a smile.

"Why not? Yes. What a great idea, Börte. It was clever of you to suggest it. And very thoughtful of you. Max will be glad."

THE MEN OF THE SS police battalion were pleased to see Max; they were pleased to see anyone who was not in the SS and who spoke their native tongue as well as the old man. Hearing him speak in German made them feel as if they were at home, which, of course, was where they all longed to be. They'd grown tired of Ukraine and the war and the crazy politics that had brought them there, not to mention the killing. Now all they wanted to do was throw away their guns and their uniforms, and go back to Germany, where they could do an honest day's work and, if such a thing was possible, pretend that none of it had ever happened.

Max understood this. But it still surprised him that men who had murdered so many men, women and children could appear so very normal—that they could laugh and joke and enjoy music like any other men. And he wondered if this was a characteristic peculiar to Germans—at least until he remembered that this was what the Soviet NKVD had been like, that they, too, had been ordinary men. Max decided that it didn't say a lot that was good about mankind in general.

"Tell us some more about Baron Falz-Fein and his family, Max," they said. "Was he really a friend of the Russian tsar?"

"Oh yes," said Max. "It's not known if he ever came to stay here with the baron. But they were friends, all right. And quite possibly related."

"What happened to the tsar?"

"To Nicholas the Second? He and his whole family were shot by the Communists. In July 1918. At a place called Yekaterinburg."

Talk of shooting whole families brought a short pause to the conversation as one or two reflected on the terrible things that they themselves had done. But finally, someone started the conversation again.

"Yekaterinburg," he said. "Is that near here?"

"No, it's a long way east of Dnepropetrovsk." Max was mentioning Dnepropetrovsk because he wanted to know if any of the men he was with now had been there. "I take it you know where that is?"

"Yes, we know where that is," said one. "We were there for a while. Carrying out special actions."

Someone else hushed the man and then offered Max a cigarette, and nervously he took it.

So, it *was* them, Max thought. It was them who had most likely murdered Kalinka's whole family, not to mention almost twenty thousand others, in the city's botanical gardens. He shuddered.

"Well," he said, controlling his revulsion, "Yekaterinburg is about twenty-five hundred kilometers east of Dnepropetrovsk."

"Twenty-five hundred?" someone gasped.

"This is a very, very big country," said Max. "So big that it seems to slip off the edge of the earth. A man could walk east all his life and still not reach the sea."

"We only just worked that out," a man said bitterly, for the madness of invading a country as large as the Soviet Union could hardly be ignored. "And the baron? What became of him? Was he shot, too?"

Max was still thinking about the horror of what had happened in Dnepropetrovsk and in many other places as well.

"What's that?" he said.

"Was the baron shot, too?"

"Er, no, just his mother, the dowager baroness. During the Bolshevik Revolution, the baron escaped back to Germany and never returned. I often wonder what became of him and his family, but I don't suppose I shall ever really know. This is not a place where you can post a letter or receive a telephone call."

All of the men nodded gloomily; it had been months since any of them had received a letter from home, and they were uncomfortably aware that a hard fight lay ahead of them if ever they were going to break through the Russian lines and get any letters that had been written to them by their families.

But a few of them were of the opinion that they were doomed and deservedly so. At this point, Captain Grenzmann, who was not one of these, spoke up:

"I believe I can answer your question, Max, about what happened to the baron," he said. "At least in part. You know that I was in the Berlin Olympics, in 1936. Well, I was checking through my sporting almanac—I'm afraid it's the only book I brought from Germany—and I came across a Falz-Fein who was in the 1936 Winter Olympics, at Garmisch-Partenkirchen. It's not exactly a common name. And I assume it must be the same family. Would you like to see the book?"

"Very much," said Max.

Captain Grenzmann took Max into the baron's old study and showed him the almanac—a great, thick book as big as a family Bible—and found the entry.

"Here we are," said the captain. "Eduard Falz-Fein."

"What? I don't believe it."

"I can assure you, it's perfectly true."

"But Eduard was born here," Max whispered, his voice choked with emotion. "September fourteen, 1912. Friedrich's first son. I remember it well."

"It seems that he was on the Liechtenstein two-man bobsled team. He'd have been, what, twenty-four? Look.

They finished in eighteenth position. Too bad. Germany in fifth and sixth, I see. Something we didn't win that year."

Max studied the entry in the book beside the captain's finger for a moment and then wiped a tear from his eye. "Good," he said finally. "I'm glad he's all right. The child born here has become a grown man. But where is Liechtenstein? And what exactly is a two-man bobsled?"

Grenzmann explained that Liechtenstein is a German-speaking country bordered by Switzerland and Austria.

"It's a principality with a constitutional monarchy," he added, "and full of people with plenty of money. Your baron must still be quite a rich fellow if his family has been living there all this time. I went skiing once in Liechtenstein. Very pretty."

Grenzmann closed the heavy book. "And a bobsled is just a large sled, only much faster than the kind of sled that children use. As well as being a rich fellow, this Eduard must be a very brave one and, to that extent at least, a typical German. Believe me, it takes a lot of guts to catapult yourself down one of these courses on one of those sleds. I did the Cresta Run on a sled at Saint Moritz once, in 1938, and I don't mind telling you, Max, it scared the living daylights out of me. Yes, I bet he and I would be great friends."

Max didn't contradict the captain but he rather doubted this: anyone who was capable of shooting a herd of almost extinct horses was not someone that any Falz-Fein could ever have called a friend.

"You know, I'm glad you came tonight, Max," said Grenzmann.

He shrugged. "Thank you for asking me," he said politely. "I'm looking forward to it."

"As I think I told you before, it's possible we may have to defend this place against the Red Army. I hope it doesn't come to that, but if it does, I should like to know the complete lay of the land. That's just good soldiering, Max. Anyway, as a result of that, I've been meaning to ask you a question."

Grenzmann beckoned Max to join him at the framed map of Askaniya-Nova on the wall of the baron's study.

"When I first arrived, you were kind enough to show me the boundaries of the reserve on this map."

"Yes, I remember."

Max went over to the map and waited patiently for the captain to explain himself.

Grenzmann grinned and pointed to a name at the bottom of the map. "Bruno Hassenstein. You can tell it was a German who made this map. It's very detailed: a scale, contours, features—a beautiful piece of work. Nevertheless, there are one or two features of this map that puzzle me."

"Oh? Such as?"

"Well, here of course is the big house, where we are now," said Grenzmann. "Here are the lakes and the local villages—even the highest point on the steppe is neatly marked. This, I think, must be your famous blue cottage. Yes, even that appears on this map. But these features here are a mystery to me. They appear to be a collection of man-made structures—you see the little squares and the two little circles?"

"Yes."

"Do you have any idea what these are?"

Max shook his head. "I'm not very good at reading maps, sir."

"But it's interesting, don't you think?"

"If you say so, sir."

Grenzmann tapped the glass covering the map with his finger. "I've looked for these structures when I've been out riding, but with no luck. Naturally, I'm reluctant to remove this map from the frame and take it with me." He shrugged. "I suppose I could make a copy. But I thought it might just be easier to ask you."

"My memory is not what it was, sir."

"And yet you had no problem remembering the date that Eduard Falz-Fein was born. That's curious, too, don't you think?"

"To be fair, the birth of a child is an important date, sir. At least it was in this house."

Max leaned toward the map and took a closer look, for form's sake. He could tell that Grenzmann was not going to let this go. The German was like a terrier with a rat when there was something on his mind. And his piercing blue eyes always seemed to hint that he knew much more than he was letting on; it was, thought Max, very unnerving.

"Now I come to think about this," he said, "I suppose it could be the ruins of an old pumping station. For water. I seem to remember that the baron made some efforts to irrigate the eastern part of the reserve. This is years ago, mind. Sorry, I'd completely forgotten about it."

"A pumping station," said Grenzmann. "That's interesting."

"Is there something wrong with the water supply in the house, sir?"

"No, Max. The water from the well here is good. In fact, I would go so far as to say it's excellent. Like I said, this was a soldier's inquiry. Please tell me more about this old pumping station."

"Let me see now, sir. It was badly damaged during the earthquake of 1927, and like a lot of things around here, it hasn't worked since. You know, there's a whole village on this map where everyone died during the great famine of 1932. You can still see it. But no one lives there." Max pointed at a place on the map. "It was here, I think."

"Yes, I've seen that village." The captain shrugged. "It's of no interest to anyone."

"That's just how it was in those days, sir. Things got built. Things were abandoned. Things are forgotten. And really, that's the story of Mother Russia."

"I wasn't asking you for a history lesson, Max. I'm a German. We don't read history; we *make* it. I was asking if you knew what these structures might be. But thank you, I think you've answered my question." He smiled.

"As I knew you would. Now let's go and eat. I could eat a horse. Which is just as well, perhaps, as that's what we're having for dinner."

Captain Grenzmann thought this was very funny and laughed a great loud laugh that Max realized was curiously like the sound of a horse whinnying.

Max tried to smile back, and then gave it up as a bad job. Whatever appetite he might have had—which wasn't much, considering what was on the menu—had been lost the moment that he'd realized he was socializing with the very men who'd murdered Kalinka's family. And now that Grenzmann had asked him about the water pumping station, he felt physically sick.

As a little girl back in Dnepropetrovsk, making paints—with cornstarch, salt, egg yolk and food colorings like cochineal, paprika, betanin, caramel and elderberry juice—had always been as much fun for Kalinka as actually painting a picture.

Her father put it differently: "Making a mess in the kitchen," he said, "seems to give my daughter more pleasure than almost anything."

Not that he ever seemed to mind all that much; besides, Kalinka always knew that she could make everything better with him by taking off his black hat—her father always wore some kind of hat, even when he was in the house—and kissing his strange-smelling head.

She didn't have any food coloring in her new home at Askaniya-Nova, but she had some tea, some egg yolk and some strawberry jam; and most important of all, she had some charcoal from the fire.

"This is going to be fun," she told Taras as she mixed her paints.

Kalinka didn't know exactly *how* those prehistoric men had painted the walls of their caves, but she knew that most of their tools had been made of flint; consequently, she imagined—correctly—that instead of brushes and palette knives, they had used their fingers for painting pictures on stone walls.

After a number of experimental palm prints on the wall—open black hands that looked like a warning of something dangerous—Kalinka tried drawing a horse with a knob of charcoal, but it needed several attempts before she got one with which she was really happy.

"The neck of a Przewalski's is much more curved than a modern horse's," she told Taras. "A bit like a hunter's bow, don't you think?"

Taras barked.

The success of these smaller paintings prompted Kalinka to be a little bolder and adventurous with her next endeavor, and working on a much larger scale seemed to inspire her to draw the outline of a really excellent horse— one that was easily good enough to color in with a shade of brown made from tea and jam, which was perfect for rendering the dun-colored body of a Przewalski's horse. This color, mixed with a little charcoal, was just right for the animal's leg stripes, mane and all-important tail.

When she was at the stage of wondering what else to do to her picture—a work of art is never finished, only ever abandoned—Kalinka walked to the opposite side of the water tank and, holding up the lamp, tried to judge her own work critically.

"What do you think, Taras?" she asked the dog.

Taras looked at the picture, inclined his head one way, then the other and wagged his tail.

In the flickering firelight, Kalinka decided the painting was pretty good—so good that she started painting another running horse almost immediately.

While she was working, Temüjin came into Kalinka's water tank to see what she was doing; his sense of another horse like him was so keen that he had felt its presence even though it was only a painting on a stone wall. The stallion stared at the picture for a full two minutes: like a cat looking at a mirror, he was fascinated with this image of himself.

Before long, Kalinka had created not just several horses running around the walls but also a reasonable imitation of a real prehistoric cave. When she compared her own efforts with the pictures in Max's book, she felt that she had exceeded her own expectations.

"Not bad," she said. "Not bad at all. Even though I say so myself. Perhaps, deep down, all painting is the same: no one ought to or can teach you how to paint the wall of a cave. It's something you can or you can't do."

Looking at her work now, Kalinka felt she had a new understanding of those ancient cavemen. She thought it was only too easy to imagine that outside her little shelter, on the windblown steppe, it was a primordial world of unimaginable harshness and severity; and in a way, of course, it was just such a world. Perhaps it was worse than that, for even at its harshest, Stone Age life was never as nasty, brutish and short as life on the Russian front. No saber-toothed tiger, woolly rhinoceros, mammoth, cave bear or Neanderthal man had ever witnessed the cruelty Kalinka had seen.

But a new thought now presented itself to her inquisitive young mind.

"You know, Taras, I wonder if it was cavemen who painted these pictures at all. Everyone assumes it was them. But why? Why couldn't it have been cave*women*? After all, it's usually the women who fix up a place and try to make it look nice. That's how it was for us back in Dnepropetrovsk. My papa was out working all day, and my mama was the one who stayed home cooking, cleaning, putting up curtains, hanging pictures and making everything neat and tidy. My papa was generally too tired to lift anything but a newspaper or his tea glass when he came home at night. It's hard to think of his Stone Age equivalent painting pictures on the walls of his cave after a day of hunting mammoth."

She shrugged.

"Either way, I can't wait to see what Max thinks of my cave. You know, it's a pity he's coming tomorrow morning, because I think these paintings look so much better at night and in the firelight. It's almost as if the horses are actually moving around the walls. If you half close your eyes, the flames seem to create the illusion that they're really running. It's a bit like going to the cinema theater. Except that these moving pictures are in color, of course. I've only ever seen movies that are in black and white."

Temüjin nodded his appreciation and allowed Kalinka to hug his back fondly, which was not something he had allowed before. Neither of them could have known that the girl's pictures were almost prophetic, and that within a matter of hours, Temüjin and Börte would be running for their lives.

Kalinka's heart skipped a beat when she heard footsteps outside the jagged stone door of the disused water tank.

"Max? Is that you?"

"Yes, it's me," he said dully, appearing in the doorway. Bearded and swathed in frosted furs, he didn't look so very different from a caveman himself.

Kalinka threw her arms around the old man and squealed with delight.

"I thought you weren't coming until tomorrow," she said.

"I—er—changed my mind." He held up a coat. "I brought you a coat, which used to belong to my wife. To help keep you warm when you go outside."

"Thank you," she said, pressing the fur on the collar to her face. "It's nice."

"It's an Astrakhan coat. I'd almost forgotten that I still

had it. It'll be a bit big, probably. But I expect you'll grow into it."

"You smell different," she observed.

Max winced. "I had a bath, that's why. Before going to dinner. And it wasn't even my birthday."

Kindly, Kalinka didn't ask him about dinner. Just by looking at his face, she could tell that the old man hadn't enjoyed it very much. She put the coat down on the floor for a moment and lifted the lantern.

"Look," she said. "I've decorated my cave."

Max glanced around and felt his own jaw drop with amazement. "Well, I never," he said. "It's incredible. They're the most beautiful paintings I think I've ever seen. And that includes the painting in my cottage that used to belong to the baron. It's wonderful what you've done in here, child. Wonderful."

He walked around the water tank, nodding his appreciation and muttering kind words of admiration. Finally, Max let out a loud laugh of delight.

"I feel just like one of those ancient cavemen seventeen thousand years ago. Whatever prompted you to do such a wonderful thing, child?"

"These old walls were a bit gray," she said. "I never liked gray all that much. And I like it a lot less since the Germans came to Ukraine. I thought that if I was going be hiding in here for a while, then it would be nice to make things a little more bright and colorful."

"Well, you've certainly done that," said Max. "You're

full of surprises." The old man tried to make his smile last awhile longer, but knowing what he knew now, this was proving to be difficult.

Mistaking his melting smile for a lack of genuine enthusiasm, Kalinka said, "I know they're a little crude. But I'll get better, and when I paint the walls of the other water tank—which is the important one—then I'm sure I'll get it just right."

"Why do you say that?" asked Max. "I think you've done a marvelous job."

"No, this was an experiment," said Kalinka. "To work out my technique. The other cave is where I'm going to do the proper work. You see, I really want to make Temüjin and Börte feel like they are outside on the steppe, with all their old friends—the horses who were shot. I might even try a few bison, too. Just like in the books you lent me."

"Well, that's very kind and thoughtful of you, Kalinka."

Temüjin nodded his affirmation of this project. He hadn't seen a lot of art, but he knew what he liked. He put his nose in Kalinka's hand for a moment, breathed warmly on the palm of her hand and then went next door to check on Börte.

Max picked up a piece of wood, dropped it onto the fire and then sat down on the floor with a heavy sigh.

"What is it, Max?" said Kalinka, sitting down beside him. "Did something awful happen when you went to see Captain Grenzmann?"

"Yes," he said. "You could say that."

"And here was I, chattering away about my stupid paintings. I should have remembered that you'd be feeling bad after—well, after, you know."

"No, it's not that," said Max. "Although that was quite bad enough. I don't think I've ever had to eat anything quite as bad as—"

Gradually, Max explained some of what had happened in the baron's old study at the big house. He did not mention that the SS men at the house were probably the same men who had killed her family.

"But what does it mean?" she asked.

"It means that bloody Captain Grenzmann won't be satisfied until he's found this place and satisfied his own curiosity that it is what I told him it was," said Max. "A ruin of no importance. It means that he might well come here as soon as tomorrow morning, when he's out riding. And I think we can guess what will happen if he finds you here. It means, my dear, dear girl, and my only true friend, that you will have to leave this place tonight. Right now. You have to go away somewhere safe. To our own Red Army lines, southeast of here."

Kalinka winced as if Temüjin had bitten her backside.

"Oh, Max," she said. "Are you sure?"

"Yes," he said. "I'm sure. And I sincerely wish I wasn't."

"I see," Kalinka said sadly. She'd been so happy in her little cave.

"Since you're without parents and without identity

papers, Kalinka, Captain Grenzmann will assume you've escaped from a camp or another special action group, and possibly shoot you at the same time as he shoots Temüjin and Börte." He sighed. "It's too bad, but there it is."

Kalinka nodded. In all other circumstances, she might have cried, but she could see Max was right and there was no point in moaning about it. Escape was now her only option.

"All right," she agreed. "Of course, I can see the sense in what you're saying. I'll go tonight." She frowned. "But look here. There's no point in me leaving here on my own. Why don't I take Temüjin and Börte with me? You said yourself, he'll shoot them if he finds them here."

He nodded. "Yes, he will."

"Think about it, Max. If they don't come with me, the breed will be extinct."

"I can't argue with that, Kalinka. But all the same, your plan is founded on the assumption that the horses will do what you say. That they'll follow you. Will they follow you? They're wild animals, after all."

"If I ask them, I think they'll come," she said. "I seem to have developed a bond with them. I'm not exactly sure why. But as I said before, I think it's because we have something in common. We're all refugees."

"Perhaps it's that, yes." Max nodded. "But I think they sense something unique in you, Kalinka. And so do I. It's a very wise head you have on very young shoulders."

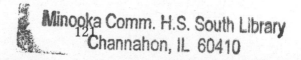

"You're wiser."

"It might seem that way, Kalinka, but no, I'm not. Wisdom is found inside the head, not in the silver beard." Max turned away. "Now, I'd better go and get some things for your journey. You stay here and see if you can work your magic with those horses and persuade them that they have to leave with you. All right?"

"All right."

As soon as Max was gone, Kalinka fetched a candle and went next door to speak to Temüjin and Börte.

The two horses had sensed something was wrong and seemed almost prepared for what she now told them.

"I need your help," she said. "It's really not safe for me in this place anymore. Most likely, the SS are coming here tomorrow and will probably kill me. Or send me to another place where someone else will kill me. But I've got a much better chance of escape if you come with me. If you want to stay here, I will understand. Askaniya-Nova is your home. It's different for me. My home is gone. Effectively, the SS destroyed that when they killed all of the Jews in Dnepropetrovsk. On the other hand, maybe you feel the same about this place. It's up to you. You decide."

Max was gone for about half an hour. When he returned, Kalinka was waiting for him with the two horses.

"What's this?" He let out a laugh. "You look like a deputation. Like you've got something to tell me."

"They're coming with me," said Kalinka.

"How do you know?" Max asked her as he put some things in the pockets of her coat and helped her put it on.

122

"I know."

"So what did you tell them?"

"They're coming because I told them I needed their help," she said. "That I don't stand much of a chance without them."

"Ah," said Max. "Makes sense, I suppose." He grinned. "Horse sense."

"I don't want to leave you, Max."

"I know. But you have to, child. Neither of us has any choice in this matter. Look here, I've given you some money—all I have. It's in the pocket of your Astrakhan coat. You'll also find a box of matches to make a fire with, a compass to help you find your way to the Red Army, and some bread and cheese. Not to mention a little something to remember me by."

"Why not come with us, Max?" She shrugged. "With all the horses gone, there's no reason for you to stay here at Askaniya-Nova."

Max shook his head. "I'm old, and I'm feeling rather tired," he said. "So I'll only slow you down. Besides, someone has to stay here and cover your tracks, so to speak." He nodded at the walls of the cave. "If Captain Grenzmann finds this lot, he'll know something is up, for sure."

"Oh," said Kalinka, looking around at her paintings sadly. "Yes, I suppose he will."

"In which case, he would certainly pursue you all. Because he's a fanatic and that's what fanatics do."

"I've given you a real problem in here, haven't I?"

"Don't you worry, Kalinka. There's nothing on these walls I can't shift with some soap and water and a stiff brush. Be a shame to clean 'em off, but that can't be helped now. One day, perhaps you'll come back here and paint them again. That's all there is to it."

"I'd like that."

"Yes, you can return with the horses. Or their descendants. After all, you're taking away a prime breeding pair." Max shook his head. "And now you really had better get going."

Kalinka pushed her hands into the pockets of the black Astrakhan coat, where they encountered the compass, the money, the bread and the cheese that he had thoughtfully placed there. The old man's kindness brought a lump to her throat. She wanted to cry but knew she couldn't. There simply wasn't any time for that sort of thing.

"It's not snowing," observed Kalinka.

Max shrugged. "What of it?"

"Captain Grenzmann will see our tracks leading away from here. And then what will happen?"

"You let me worry about that, child."

"But he might shoot you, too, Max. Have you thought of that? I couldn't bear the thought of this happening to you."

"I'll be fine. He thinks he's my friend, remember? Give me the compass."

Max showed her how to read the compass and then gave it back to her.

"Now listen to me: you should always be going south-east, toward the Reds," he said. "There's plenty of moon-light, so you won't have any problem reading it tonight. To the north are Captain Grenzmann and his detachment of SS—not to mention Dnepropetrovsk; and to the west is the whole German army. So above all, steer clear of northwest. If you lose the compass, just walk toward the rising sun. Clear?"

Kalinka restrained a yawn and then nodded.

"I know you're tired," said Max. "But there's no time to lose sleeping. Besides, the cold will wake you up. You and the horses need to put as much distance as you can between yourselves and this place before morning. And then to keep going all day if you can, before resting. Don't worry about the horses. They're tough as nails and can walk forever. Just remember that. If they stop, it will only be because they think it's you that's tired."

Max and Taras and Kalinka and the two Przewalski's went outside the water tank, along the brick passageway past the pumping room, and through the hidden entrance to the outside, where the wind on the open steppe took her breath away.

Max knelt down beside Taras in the snow and hugged the dog for a moment.

"Go with her, Taras," he said. "Go with Kalinka and see that no harm comes to her."

Taras barked his obedience and stood next to Kalinka. Max rose stiffly.

"Max, no," she protested. "I couldn't take your dog."

"He's getting fat and lazy, staying here with me," said Max. "Aren't you, boy? You'd be doing him a kindness to take him with you, young lady. He's a borzoi—a wolfhound. Wasn't bred to be a pet, which is what he's become. This is just what a dog like him needs. A proper steppe-sized adventure. Like something from a great novel by Gogol. He won't get that if he stays here with an old man like me at Askaniya-Nova. He's a good dog. You only have to tell him anything once, and I've told him now—to go with you, Kalinka—so there's no going back on it and that's an end to the matter."

"God bless you, Max," she said, and embraced him. "I shan't ever forget you. Not if I live to be a hundred."

Max kissed her forehead and then walked quickly toward his cottage. There was much to do before morning.

EVEN INSIDE HER BIG black Astrakhan coat, Kalinka felt bitterly cold; the wind was from the north and behind her. Temüjin and Börte, following in her footsteps, managed to screen the girl from the worst of the bora wind, but even so, the night was soon in her bones, as if she had fallen through a sheet of ice and into the dark water of a freezing lake. The tattered lining of her coat was made of red silk, and she found it almost funny that she could be swathed in red and yet still feel blue with cold.

"If we can keep up this pace until dawn," said Kalinka, "then maybe we stand a chance. I know we're leaving a trail in the snow that's going to be very easy to follow, but there's not much we can do about that. And if we hear motors coming after us, then you horses should run in opposite directions. Have you got that?"

From time to time, she brought out the little brass compass and took a bearing in the way that Max had shown her—just to make sure that they were headed in the right direction. The strange quartet made good progress, for the snow was only a few centimeters deep on the steppe and the ground was more or less flat. After a couple of hours, she guessed they'd walked at least ten kilometers.

The bread and cheese felt good in her pocket, and she decided to put off eating them for as long as possible; experience had taught Kalinka that she was never as hungry if she knew there was food she could eat than when she had no idea of where her next meal was coming from.

At first, Kalinka spoke to the dog and to the horses to try to keep up her spirits, but every time she said something, she saw her hot breath appear before her face in a little white cloud of steam, and she soon realized that talk was an easy way to lose body heat. And so, after a while, she said nothing at all. Besides, it was easier to hear things when you weren't talking.

Not that hearing things was always a good thing.

Once, she heard what sounded like a lion roaring in the distance, and it was several heart-stopping moments before she managed to remember that there weren't any lions in Ukraine and that what she could actually hear was the sound of a European bison bull bellowing his heart out. All the same, she was glad there wasn't much light and that she couldn't see the bison and that he couldn't see her.

Another time, she heard a strange whooping noise, and it was the next day before she was able to connect this strange sound with some zebras, the sight of which was unnerving to her, because she was certain that zebras existed only in Africa, like lions, and it occurred to her that if there were zebras at Askaniya-Nova, then there might just as easily be lions, too.

Strangest of all was the noise of a llama—another animal she was sure existed on a different continent. This sounded exactly like someone laughing his head off, and she almost thought it might be a hyena, until she saw the llama, which was as white as the snow and, in the bright moonlight, resembled a creature from a fairy tale.

All of these noises were made less alarming to Kalinka by the fact that Taras, the dog, and Temüjin and Börte seemed not in the least bit bothered by them. And the only time the three animals stopped and pricked up their ears was when they heard what Kalinka was quite certain was a wolf howling in the distance.

Now, as anyone will tell you, a howling wolf is a wonderful sound, but only if you are inside a warm house with a lock on the door. It is not a sound you want to hear when you are standing in the middle of an open steppe in winter—especially, as on this occasion, when the wolf's plaintive howl received a swift reply from another wolf.

"Wolves," whispered Kalinka. "Max didn't say there would be wolves, Taras." She made a fist inside her coat pocket. "This is a good start to our journey."

Taras stayed silent; he was too busy listening to bark at the girl. And besides, he hardly wanted to give their exact position away to the wolves, although he had a good idea that they had already picked up their scent—not that this was difficult. There wasn't one of them—the girl included—who didn't smell as strongly as a nest of mice.

"Perhaps I should light a fire," whispered Kalinka, fingering the box of matches in her coat pocket. "Wolves don't like fire. Not that there's wood or anything else to put a match to." She thought for a moment. "Perhaps if I gave them the bread and the cheese? No, I thought not. A hungry wolf is hardly likely to make do with a cheese sandwich, is he?"

Taras glanced at her impatiently; then they heard another yowling howl, and this time it seemed much, much closer. Taras looked at Kalinka uncertainly. He was sure the horses could defend themselves, but about the girl he was much less sure. Without a doubt, she was the weakest in their group, and her soft white flesh would look all too inviting to a leaping wolf. If only the old man had thought to give her a walking stick, then at least she might have used it to hit something.

"I wish dear Max was here with his gun," she whispered. "Better still, I wish I was back in his little blue cottage."

A minute passed, and none of the animals beside the girl moved or made a sound. All Kalinka could hear was the cold bora wind moaning over the snow-covered grass and her own nervous breathing. The silence was even more unnerving than the howl of the wolves, for she realized that it meant something ominous now.

Slowly, Taras turned around to face the direction where they'd heard the wolf's howl coming from; so did Temüjin, and Kalinka sensed that something was about to happen that only the three animals who were her companions actually understood.

"Are they going to attack, do you think?" she asked the dog. "I've never even seen a wolf, and I don't know what to do. Should I crouch down? Should I play dead?"

Taras lowered his tense body, growled and pinned his small ears back so that he resembled a wolf himself. He was a big dog: at the shoulder, he was as high as a man's waist, but the girl doubted he was equal to a contest with a pack of wolves. And even though Taras was a wolfhound, she had the idea that when borzois hunted wolves, they did it not on their own but in pairs. Besides, he had such a gentle-looking face, it was hard to imagine him fighting anything.

Meanwhile, the stallion lifted his furry tail and his head, showed his big yellow teeth to the moon and let out a strange noise that was part snort and part growl—a blustering sound that was full of aggression and determination to stand his ground against whatever the night now threw at him.

131

Bright eyes shifted in the dark like fireflies. Kalinka's chest felt so tight, she could hardly breathe. There were at least two wolves circling them, patiently looking for the weakest one of the four travelers to attack. That is how it always is with wolves. Stealth and patience and, above all, a ruthless drive to kill; in that respect, at least, they reminded Kalinka of the Nazis. She swallowed her fear and tried not to let it show, for she had an idea that wolves can smell terror. She was right. Taras pushed out his chest and barked fiercely at the bright eyes, and for a moment, they disappeared.

Kalinka had discovered the special fear of wolves. Everyone has it. It's a fear that goes right back to the time when man lived in caves and painted horses on the walls by firelight and very sensibly avoided the forests and open steppe at night.

Taras stared hard into the darkness; every fiber of his being was on guard against imminent attack. Temüjin clopped the hard snow with one hoof, ready to smash a wolf's skull if that was what was required, while Börte patrolled in a circle around Kalinka.

"I can't see anything," she whispered. "Have they gone?"

The next second, three, or perhaps four, wolves arrived at a sprint from opposite directions with the same object in mind: to catch the girl by the throat and then hang on long enough to bring her down and kill her, at which point they estimated that the dog and the horses would have no choice but to abandon her body.

With jaws bared viciously, the first wolf—a big male—launched himself like a streak of snarling gray lightning at the girl, only to be met by a perfectly judged double kick from Temüjin as both the stallion's rear hooves lashed out in unison and connected very solidly with the wolf's body; the hapless animal flew through the air with an injured yelp and landed somewhere in the darkness, whereupon Temüjin gave immediate chase with the intention of trampling the wolf to death. But although badly stunned, the wolf still had sufficient presence of mind to pick himself up and run away as quickly as he could.

The second wolf—a female—fared even worse than her mate, for it was not Kalinka's throat that ended up being gripped in a pair of powerful jaws but the wolf's own, as hundreds of years' breeding in the big white wolfhound suddenly came to the fore. With a loud snap, Taras caught the animal expertly as she sprang at the girl and, holding the wolf tightly, shook her hard, several times, as if she were no bigger than a rat. He might have held on to her, too, but for the fact that Börte bit the wolf on one back leg and then the other, which was so painful and made the wolf writhe so much that she twisted herself free and limped quickly away before the horse or the dog could bite her again.

Temüjin snapped his jaws shut on an ear and then a

tail, and in the darkness, something gray and furry let out an agonized yelp; he lashed out behind him with his rear hooves and felt a dull thud as they connected with the wolf he had just bitten.

Breathlessly, Taras and the two Przewalski's turned one way and then the other, instinctively searching for more wolves; the dog barked loudly, as if challenging any others to come forward and pit themselves against dog and wild horse, but there was none. Sensing victory, Temüjin rose up on his hind legs and cycled his front hooves in the air; at the same time, he let out a loud neigh that was nothing short of triumphant.

When the second wolf had attacked, Kalinka had ducked down abruptly and then slipped on the snow; for the few seconds it had lasted, she had watched the fight lying down, as she thought it best to stay out of the way.

She was still lying there now, and Taras wasn't sure if the girl had been injured or not. Almost immediately after the danger was past, he came over to check that she was all right. Kalinka took his long, almost curved muzzle in her hands and hugged the dog's head close to her body.

"Thank you," she said as the dog licked her face fondly. "You were so brave, Taras."

She stood up and hugged the bodies of both horses.

"You too, Temüjin. You saved my life. And you, Börte. Thank you so much. I told you that I couldn't do this without you." She let out a breath that was part relief and part fear, and shivered. "But for the three of you—well, I've a good idea how Little Red Riding Hood must have felt. I just wish I had a treat to give to you all."

She glanced up at the moon. "Come on," she said. "There's no time to waste. Southeast is this way."

THAT NIGHT, MAX PRAYED for it to snow to cover the tracks of Kalinka and the Przewalski's horses, which led away from the old waterworks like a trail of bread crumbs, but no snow came—not so much as a flake. Max started to brush over the tracks, but this simply made their trail bigger and more obvious. He racked his brains for an idea as to how he might cover them effectively but none came. Finally, he decided that if he were asked about the tracks by Grenzmann, he would have to tell the German SS captain that the tracks had probably been made by deer or llamas; there were still a few around that the Germans had not killed and eaten.

If there wasn't much that Max could do about concealing a suspicious-looking trail in the snow, there was something he could do about Kalinka's "cave paintings," and the old man reluctantly decided to clean the paintings off the walls of the water tank—just in case the captain turned up and put two and two together about what and perhaps who had been staying there. So as soon as he had given up trying to cover the trail of Kalinka and the horses, Max trudged back to his cottage to fetch a bucket, a broom, a brush and some soap flakes, and, returning immediately to the water tank, began to try to scrub the walls clean of evidence.

It wasn't long before he made an uncomfortable discovery: the paintings could not be removed from the stone wall of the water tank. Try as he might—and he tried all night long—the best of them remained indelibly all around the circular wall, as if they'd been there for thousands of years. Soap and water and huge amounts of scrubbing, which left Max lathered in sweat, had absolutely no effect on Kalinka's perfect little black palm prints and her excellent paintings of the Przewalski's horses. At first, Max was puzzled that something so new could prove to be so indestructible; if it hadn't been inconvenient to his plans, he might even have said it was a miracle that Kalinka's paintings should prove to be as durable as the French ones, and it was several hours before the old man worked out exactly what must have happened. Unwittingly, the girl had created a perfect fresco painting: her homemade colors, mixed with water, had been applied to a damp stone surface; these pigments had been absorbed by the stone and then quickly dried by the wood fire that was still burning on the floor, so that the paintings were now as permanently fixed in the very fabric of the wall as if they had been painted on the ceiling of the great cathedral in Kiev. "That's torn it, Taras," said Max, quite forgetting for a moment that he had told his faithful dog to go with Kalinka and the horses. "If this situation wasn't so dangerous, it might be funny."

So he had to content himself with burning her old coat and the books with the cave pictures of the horses, and sweeping away some horse dung.

"With any luck, that captain will take my word about this place and not come here at all," the old man told his absent dog. "I mean, it's just an old waterworks, after all is said and done—not a weapons arsenal or a Red Army barracks. It makes no sense to be suspicious of absolutely everything, like he is."

But in his bones, Max knew that Grenzmann wasn't the type to accept anyone's word for anything—least of all someone who was not German. And he knew that as soon as the captain saw the paintings, his life at Askaniya-Nova would become very awkward indeed—and quite possibly worse than that, since he knew the SS didn't take kindly to being made fools of. He suspected that the same thing that had happened in the botanical gardens at Dnepropetrovsk would now happen to him.

"That doesn't matter," he told himself, for by now he had remembered that Taras had gone with Kalinka. "What matters is that they make their escape and start a new life somewhere else."

When he was satisfied he had done all he could—he left the fire burning, to make sure that Kalinka's old coat was properly consumed by the flames—Max went back into the brick passageway, past the pumping station, and opened the secret door that led outside onto the steppe.

An unpleasant but hardly unexpected discovery awaited him: it was Grenzmann on his tall Hanoverian horse, with four of his SS men seated on two motorcycles and in their sidecars.

"Max," said Grenzmann. "This is a surprise. And, then again, perhaps not such a surprise." Smiling thinly, he jumped down from the horse and walked toward the old man. "Here we all are, looking for the entrance to the baron's old waterworks, and all of a sudden there you are, showing us exactly where to find it. How about that?"

"After you mentioned it last night, sir," explained Max, his heart pounding, "I decided to come and have a look at the place myself. To see if there was anything I could scavenge. And in case, at a later date, you wanted me to show you around."

Grenzmann grinned and wagged his finger at the old man. "You know, you're such a bad liar, Max," he said. "I don't know why I put up with it. Really, I don't. I give you my friendship—we invite you to supper—and this is how you repay our trust: with lies and evasions. It's really quite intolerable. If your German wasn't so perfect, I might be tempted to shoot you right here and now."

Max shook his head and then snatched off his cap. "It's not like that at all, sir. I told you the plant was useless, and it is."

"Don't split hairs with me, Max. It's obvious that you are hiding something in there. The question is, what? Or perhaps who? But I think we're going to find out."

"I can assure you, sir, that there's no one here except you and me and these men."

"Perhaps that's true now," admitted the captain. "But these tracks, leading away from here to the horizon, suggest that it wasn't true a while ago—until last night, perhaps, when I first mentioned this place to you and you were so hopelessly evasive."

"Tracks, sir?"

The captain came and grabbed Max by the collar of his coat and led him to the trail, where he pushed the old man onto the snow. "These tracks," he said. "The ones that lead to the southeast of here."

Grenzmann frowned.

"Now look what you made me do. You made me lose my temper. I very much dislike losing my temper, Max. What is it someone said? 'When you lose your temper, you lose the argument'? Not that this is much of an argument. I mean, we both know I'm right and that you're lying."

"Ah, you mean those tracks."

"Yes, I do mean those tracks."

"I hardly noticed them, sir. They look like deer tracks.

I think there are still a few on the reserve that your men have not yet killed."

Grenzmann laughed. "Really, it's amusing. I have to hand it to you, Max. You are a most persistently stubborn fellow. You insult me with your lies. I think we both know that these tracks in the snow are not the tracks of a deer—which has two toes that make an upside-down heart shape—but the tracks of a small horse, which has no toes. Do you really think it's possible that an Olympic equestrian like me—someone who's been around horses all his life—would not recognize the hoofprint of a horse? To be more exact—two small horses, not to mention the tracks of a dog—your dog—*and a human being*. And this is the intriguing part: whose tracks are *these*? A partisan, perhaps? A Red Army soldier? Who?" He shrugged. "Well, perhaps we'll find out more when we go inside the waterworks, if that's what this is. I'm no longer sure about anything you've told me." He looked at one of his men. "Bring him along," he said coldly.

With Max now their prisoner, the Germans went through the hidden door and along the passageway. While two of the captain's men inspected the mechanics of the pumping station, the captain and two others walked out the other side and into one of the stone water tanks, where the captain sniffed the air suspiciously.

"It smells very much like horse in here, Max." Picking up the broom, Grenzmann turned it around and put his nose near the head. "No question about it," he added.

"Horse." He smiled. "A horse that knows how to open a door and sweep up its own dung, perhaps."

"Sir," said a voice from inside the other water tank. "Come and take a look at this."

Everyone went through the jagged doorway of the second tank, where an SS sergeant had lit a lantern and was lifting it above his head to illuminate Kalinka's paintings.

Grenzmann took the lantern from his sergeant and was silent for a moment as he looked around the stone wall.

"Remarkable," he said eventually. "Quite remarkable. And really very artistic. Exactly like being in one of those French caves at Lascaux. You haven't heard of those, Max? Yes, they're a recent discovery in Vichy France. I read about that in a newspaper. Apparently, they're at least seventeen thousand years old. Although I'll hazard a guess that these on your walls are not nearly so old. I'll also guess that these are not the work of some primitive Stone Age man but of someone rather more contemporary." He bent down beside one of Kalinka's black palm prints and placed his own hand over it. "And altogether smaller. Most likely a child. Or a young woman. How about it, Max? Has someone been living in here, in secret?"

"Only very recently," admitted Max. "And quite without my knowledge. As a matter of fact, it was only yesterday I discovered—quite by chance—that someone was living in here."

"That remains to be seen," said Grenzmann. He rubbed at one of the black palm prints with a gloved hand. "I must say, these handprints don't look like they were done only yesterday. They seem quite indelible."

"I can assure you, I'm telling you the truth, sir. And, really, it was so cold, I could hardly throw this person out onto the steppe."

"And those sub-equine Przewalski's horses of yours. Were they also here without your knowledge? This is your last chance to level with me."

"No, sir. I brought them here."

"How many?"

"Two."

"Two stallions? Two mares? One of each? What are we talking about?"

Max might have been more careful about how he answered this question if he had known just how far the SS captain was prepared to go in carrying out his orders.

"A stallion and a mare," he said.

"So. A breeding pair. Perhaps the last two on the estate. Maybe even in the world."

"I couldn't bear to see them slaughtered like all the others," said Max.

"Max," said the captain sadly. "I told you. I had strict orders from my superiors in Berlin. The Przewalski's horses are an altogether inferior species of Gypsy-like horses that must be liquidated. So as to prevent the domestic horse from being contaminated with their blood.

You can see why that's necessary, surely? If your stinking Przewalski's horses were allowed to breed with decent domestic horses, they might affect the whole bloodline; it might even become impossible to domesticate horses at all. And then where would we be? I was quite clear about this matter, was I not?"

"Yes, sir," admitted Max.

"All the same," said Grenzmann. "I suppose that's almost forgivable, under the circumstances, you having been here so long."

"Thank you, sir."

"The horses will be tracked down and eliminated, of course. I have no choice in that matter. I have my orders and I'm obliged to carry them out. Come what may. Especially now that I know this is a pair capable of breeding. Yes, that makes things different. All of our earlier efforts to liquidate this breed will have been for nothing if they manage to reproduce."

Grenzmann frowned.

"But what disturbs me more is that there was someone else here, looking after these horses. Someone about whom I have no knowledge. I don't like that. I don't like that at all. It smacks of subversion."

"I can assure you, sir, that this person was absolutely no threat to you and your men." He shrugged. "Otherwise I would never have let them stay here."

"Hmm. I wish I could believe that."

"Sir," said the SS sergeant, and kicking the fire out,

he bent down and retrieved the remains of Kalinka's old coat from the embers. "It looks as if someone has been trying to burn the evidence of their being here. This looks like a coat."

Instinctively—he was, after all, a kind of policeman—the sergeant started to search the pockets of the smoldering coat. He found a piece of foil in which Max's chocolate had been wrapped, a few buttons, a coin and a carefully folded piece of yellow material that Kalinka had been saving as a souvenir of her dreadful experiences. The sergeant handed the material to the captain and then glanced sadly at Max, for he knew what this meant for the old man's prospects. While a scrap of poor-quality yellow material would normally have told someone very little, this particular piece of yellow material was eloquence itself—especially to SS men like the sergeant and Captain Grenzmann—for it was by now obvious that the material had been cut off the coat's breast pocket. But it was the shape of the material that everyone recognized immediately and that changed Max's fortunes irrevocably.

It was a yellow Star of David.

KALINKA WAS TREMBLING INSIDE her Astrakhan coat for almost an hour after the wolf attack; it was as if she'd had an electric shock, and although she had not slept in more than twenty-four hours, she now felt wide awake. This was just as well, as there was still a long way to go before they were safely off the steppe, and when the dawn came to expose their insignificance in that vast, open space, Kalinka saw quickly just how vulnerable they were. There was nowhere to hide—not a tree nor a bit of shrubbery nor a dip behind a hill that might have concealed them from anyone in pursuit. What was worse, a blind man could have followed their trail: the tracks in the snow were like some evil serpent that continually threatened to betray them. Every time she turned to look at their tracks, what she saw made her feel almost sick.

"If only it would snow again," said Kalinka, eyeing

their trail uncomfortably. "Or if only it could get a little warmer and the existing snow would melt. Then we might feel sure that no one could follow us. But so long as that trail exists, then so does the possibility that the Germans will follow it."

Taras barked and kept on walking.

"I'm sorry. You're quite right. That kind of talk doesn't do any good at all, does it? But I can't help feeling nervous when I see exactly where we have come from. Every minute, I'm convinced we're going to see the Germans coming after us on their motorcycles. If only this were Egypt, they might run into one of those ten plagues."

The wind stiffened a little, and momentarily Kalinka was grateful that it was not blowing in her face, which might have made the going slower; even so, it was clear that she was the slowest of the four, and every so often, Taras would stop and look around at her, patiently waiting for her to catch up.

"Yes, I can see what you're thinking, Taras. You're thinking, 'If only she could walk a little faster.' Now I've got you doing it. My father used to say that unless you're careful, a lot of *if onlys* can add up to one long, hard-luck story. But it's me who's slowing you all down, isn't it? If only Temüjin and Börte weren't wild horses, then perhaps I could ride and then we'd make much better progress. We could cover twice as much ground in half the time. I guess it's just my luck to be guiding wild horses to safety instead of tame ones." She shrugged.

"Then again, if you weren't the rarest horses in the world and probably the last of your kind, there would be no point in guiding you to safety at all. Each of you would be just another tall horse like that big dumb Hanoverian."

Taras barked again and shot an accusing sort of glance at Temüjin. It had been easy enough for the wild horse to avoid the dog's eye in the darkness, but now, in dawn's cold and unforgiving light, this was more difficult. The stallion knew exactly what the dog was thinking, and there was no getting away from what was obviously the right thing to do.

Temüjin walked ahead of Börte, herded the mare to a halt and then gave Taras a sideways look. He glanced back at the trail for a moment and then snorted at the girl, which sounded awfully like a sigh. Kalinka was strong but slow—that could hardly be denied—and the solution was obvious. The dog was right about that. Their survival was going to require compromises from them—perhaps Temüjin most of all.

Now, some of the buttons on the girl's Astrakhan coat were missing, and wound twice around her narrow waist was a long black leather belt that Max had tied there to help keep the coat closed against the cold wind; after a moment or two's further consideration of the matter at hand, the stallion stepped forward and nibbled at Kalinka's buckle.

"Hey, stop it," she said. "This is no time to play, Temüjin. Taras is right. We have to get going again. If they catch us out here in the middle of the steppe, we're all sitting ducks. And you know what happens to sitting ducks when there are men with guns around."

Temüjin swung his head and then stamped the ground impatiently; then he nibbled the buckle again.

"You want this belt?" she asked. "Why?" But she took it off anyway and let the stallion take it in his mouth. "All right. Have it. But I don't understand. You can't eat it. Or maybe you can; I really don't know what a wild horse can eat." She shrugged. "I saw a goat eat a shoe once. And that was made of leather. I guess if a goat can eat something that's made of leather, then maybe a wild horse can, too. Maybe you're just hungrier than I think you are."

Temüjin took the belt and laid his head across Börte; when he moved away again, the belt remained lying on Börte's neck.

By now it was clear to Kalinka that Temüjin wasn't going to eat the belt, but the cold had numbed the space between her ears and it was several seconds before she understood what was being suggested.

"Wait a minute," she said. "You want me to buckle this around Börte's neck?"

Taras barked and wagged his long, curved tail; he understood, even if the girl was being a bit slow about this.

"Temüjin? Are you suggesting I should ride Börte?"

Temüjin nodded and then nudged Kalinka toward the mare.

"I'm sorry, Temüjin. If I sound surprised, that's only

because I am. I thought you Przewalski's were the only true horses never to have been domesticated. At least that's what Max told me. But hold on a second—what does Börte have to say about it? Shouldn't we ask her permission or something? I mean, it seems a bit rude just to climb on her back without so much as a by-your-leave."

The mare reached around, took Kalinka's coat in her mouth and pulled the girl gently toward her.

"All right, all right. I understand. You're okay with this." She buckled the belt around Börte's neck and then prepared to mount. "I'll give it a try. After all, they say that even a bear can be taught to dance, so maybe this will work. I don't mind admitting to you that my feet are beginning to ache; they're also very wet and very cold. But if this is some kind of Przewalski's joke, then I'm not going to be at all amused. There's a time and a place for a joke, and take my word for it, this just isn't it. Believe me, I left all of my sense of humor back in Dnepropetrovsk. After what happened there, I may never laugh again."

Kalinka took hold of her makeshift bridle and then leapt up onto the mare's broad back; a little to her surprise, the wild horse did not try to throw her off.

"Well, I never," she said. "I guess you're only really wild when you want to be, huh?" She nodded as Börte began to walk steadily, as if the horse was quite used to having a rider on her back. "Well, this is better. I like it up here. And I can also see farther in all directions. Not that there's anything very much to see. But you get the idea. That might come in useful."

"Oh, I wish I had a camera so that I could send Max a picture. He would never believe this. I can hardly believe it myself. I'm really riding a wild horse. But look, I promise never to let any other wild horses know that this happened. All right? I can see how that might be a little embarrassing for horses like you."

Taras barked and picked up the pace immediately, and so did the two Przewalski's horses.

Kalinka took a tighter hold of Börte's simple bridle, squeezed her thighs against the mare's flanks and, before long, all three were running across the steppe.

"This is great!" she yelled. "Clever old you, Temüjin, for suggesting this."

Taras looked at Temüjin and growled in disgust, as if to say, "Yes, clever old you, Temüjin."

CAPTAIN GRENZMANN LOOKED AT the scorched yellow cloth star that the sergeant had given him and nodded gravely.

Everything was clear to him now—it was clear what had been going on, and it was equally clear what he was going to have to do about it. Not that he wanted to do anything very much about it, of course, but what choice did he have? There were strict orders from Berlin about what to do in situations like the one that now presented itself. Under the circumstances, he had no alternative but to act, and act harshly. That was the discipline the SS lived by. Without that, they were nothing, just a rabble. His men knew that, too. They liked Max as much as he did, but he could see that they already knew what was going to happen.

Grenzmann took off his battered gray hat and rubbed the short blond hair on his head slowly, almost as if he was hoping to make his twisted Nazi brain find another solution to the problem that was in front of him. In fact, he was rubbing his scalp because it delayed him from striking the old man, which was his first inclination on seeing the yellow star. It was odd how that made everything so very different; but for this simple insignia, he could probably have ignored all of the old man's many misdemeanors. The orders from his superiors were crystal clear about this sort of thing, however; retribution was absolute. There could be no room for maneuvering.

All Kaspar Grenzmann wanted to do in the world was ride horses, paint pictures, listen to Mozart and help his father run the business in his hometown of Munich. Before the war, he had been studying to become a lawyer, and he thought of himself as a gentle, civilized man. But there was nothing civilized about what he and hundreds of men like him had been asked to do all over eastern Europe. He knew that it was highly unlikely he would ever feel civilized again. But what could he do? This foolish old man had pushed him into a dark corner where he had no choice but to behave ruthlessly and without mercy—to be that which he was increasingly reluctant to be: the inflexible SS man of blood and honor.

Finally, the irritation of this realization was too much for Grenzmann and he hit the old man hard on the side of the head with the back of his gloved hand; it wasn't hard enough to knock him over, but it was hard enough to make Grenzmann feel a little ashamed of himself.

"You foolish old man," he said through clenched teeth.

"Now look at what you made me do. You see? Everything is different now between you and me. It didn't have to be like this, Max. But you have painted me on your wall. I am fixed there like one of those blasted horses. Me and what I am now required to do. Which is my duty, of course. I have no alternative now but to punish you."

Grenzmann clenched his fist for a moment and turned away for fear of hitting the old man again. He took a deep breath, let it out and then turned back to face him.

"I'm sorry," he sighed wearily, "for losing my temper like that. It was unforgivable. And let me add that it gives me absolutely no pleasure to find myself obliged to act here, but you leave me no choice. You know that, don't you? I've given you every chance, wouldn't you say? But you seem intent on betraying my trust. First, the Przewalski's horses, and now this. Really, it's too much, Max. I'm very disappointed. Honestly, I thought we were friends."

Max wiped his mouth and found a little blood on the back of his gnarled hand, which seemed to make him realize something, too: that the time had surely come to tell the young German officer the truth—not about Kalinka and where she had come from, but about the captain himself and his being there at Askaniya-Nova.

"No," he said quietly. "You were deluded. We were never friends, you and I, Captain. How could I be friends with a man like you—a man who has systematically tried to destroy everything I hold dear in this world? Not just the people who lived peacefully in this country but also the animals that lived on this great nature reserve at Askaniya-Nova. How could I be friends with a monster like you, Captain? You and your men have made everything ugly by your presence here in Ukraine. And I pity you as I would pity a man-eating bear—as something that needs to be destroyed for the good of everyone. Friend? No. I'm sure we can both spell it, Captain Grenzmann. Even in German. But only I know what it means."

Grenzmann nodded and then glanced at the sergeant.

"Take him outside," he said quietly.

In the cold dawn, Grenzmann mounted his horse, and the SS men sat in the sidecars of their motorcycles and checked that their heavy machine guns were loaded, the way they'd done many times before. The guns weren't pointed at Max.

"Walk over there a bit," Grenzmann told the old man.

Max started to walk; there was no point in running. Where could he have gone? Besides, the motorcycles would have caught up with him in seconds.

"Stop where you are," said Grenzmann. "That will do fine where you are now."

Max took off his cap, knelt down on the snow and crossed himself carefully in the Russian way. It was a while since he'd said a proper prayer, so he didn't bother; he told himself that God had certainly made up his mind one way or the other where Max was concerned.

The old man glanced up at the sky and marveled at the beauty of the Ukrainian landscape. It was such a magical place. For a moment, he remembered how, in spring, the deer would eat the heads of the magnolias outside his little cottage when they were still in bud, just as the goats ate the blue irises on the steppe—greedily, for they must have known they were too hot for their mouths—and how sometimes Max had to chase them both off because of what he now considered to be the sheer selfishness of wanting to see these flowers resplendent in all their glory. If the rest of the world was as lovely as Askaniya-Nova when the flowers were out, there was much to be thankful for. He took a deep breath of the cold air and smiled quietly at how good it made him feel. And gradually his smile broadened, until all of the Germans could see it. This left them feeling very awkward indeed.

"I don't know what you're smiling about, Max," said Grenzmann. "When this is over, we're going in pursuit of your friends: the horses, the dog and your little refugee. That won't be too difficult; after all, they've left a trail as wide as a railway track. And when we catch up with them, well, you can imagine what's going to happen. The same thing that's going to happen to you now."

Max pointed at the sun and laughed. "Do you see that sun?" he asked the captain. "And that beautiful blue sky? I reckon it's going to be warmer than it was yesterday. In a couple of hours, that snow will melt. And so will their trail. With any luck, they'll be off the steppe by dinnertime."

He heard the guns being loaded, and nodded. He was ready.

"I doubt that very much," said Grenzmann.

"You know, I've just had an idea, Captain. When all this is over. I mean, when you've done your worst here to me, why don't you get your pen and paper and draw a picture? Of my dead body. You're good at drawing. So why not combine that with the only other thing you're good at?"

The captain swallowed uncomfortably, as if the old man's words had stuck in his throat. He glanced at his men and raised his arm.

"Any last words, Max?"

"Yes." Max had thought of a poem he'd learned as a boy at school. "Ukraine is not yet dead."

"Maybe not," said the captain. "But you are."

THEY MADE GOOD, STEADY progress, although it
wasn't very long before the insides of Kalinka's
thighs started to ache and she wished she'd had a saddle
and some stirrups so that she could have stood up now
and then to stretch her legs. But she said nothing to her
companions because she was not the type to complain,
and besides, the alternative—walking—was infinitely
more inconvenient.

The sun came up, and the sky turned a brilliant shade
of bright blue that seemed to tint the snow. The air got
much warmer; steam plumed off the horses' big bodies.
From time to time, Kalinka looked around to see how
their snow trail was faring, in the hope that it might just
melt away, but it was still there, like a tail even longer
than the dog's that she couldn't get rid of.

Ahead of the two horses, Taras made the pace like

the lead dog in a team of huskies; he didn't seem to tire, and Kalinka marveled that he was never distracted by an interesting smell on the steppe: a rabbit or a hare. Perhaps there were no rabbits or hares—Max had told her that game was in short supply that winter—but even so, she thought it impressive that any dog could be quite so single-minded. Taras just kept trotting on as if he had an important mission to accomplish, which of course he did: Max had charged him with the survival of the girl, and Taras meant to accomplish this or die in the attempt.

A couple of hours passed, and the dog and the two horses slowed to a steady walk and, gradually, the gentle motion of the mare and the sun on her head took hold of Kalinka's sleep-deprived senses. Slowly, she allowed her eyes to close against the bright glare of the snow and, for a blissful moment, she dreamed that she was safe, back home in Dnepropetrovsk with her whole family.

Her father and brothers were already out on a round, delivering coal, while her mother was making *oladushki*— buttermilk pancakes—for Kalinka's breakfast. Served with a selection of sour cream, jam and maple syrup, *oladushki* were Kalinka's favorite breakfast. She often made them herself but, try as she might, the ones she cooked never tasted quite as delicious as the ones her mother made.

"Why is that?" she had asked. "Why don't my pancakes taste as good as yours, Mama?"

"Because when I'm cooking them for you, I use an extra ingredient that you don't," said her mother.

Kalinka was cross. "That's not fair," she said. "Using a secret ingredient puts me at a real disadvantage when I'm making my own *oladushki*. A little salt, maybe? A special kind of flour? Tell me."

"I didn't say it was a secret ingredient," said her mother. "I just said that I used it when I was making *oladushki* for you, Kalinka. And one day, when you're cooking for your own family, maybe you'll see how this is what makes all the difference."

"So what is it? Please, I want to know."

"It's something I always use when I'm cooking pancakes for you and your brothers and sisters, or buckwheat kasha for your father. Love. I make everything with love, Kalinka. In my experience, that always makes things taste a lot better."

And somehow it was true—the cakes your own mother bakes always taste better than . . .

Kalinka awoke with a start. She didn't know how long she had dozed but it couldn't have been for very long. Börte had stopped in her tracks and so had Temüjin; it was another moment or two before she saw the reason both horses had pulled up was that Taras had come to an abrupt halt ahead of them. The dog's long white face was lifted up toward the sun, and she could hear him noisily sampling the air with his shiny black nose.

In silence, they all waited for the dog's keen sense of smell and even keener hearing to work to their advantage.

"What is it, Taras?" she whispered. "Wolves again?"

Glad of an excuse to dismount, Kalinka jumped down from Börte's back and approached the big wolfhound.

"D'you smell danger?"

Slowly, the dog's long tail curled between his back legs, and his body started to tremble. Then Taras sat down on the cold, snowy steppe and began to chew the air like it was a solid thing, and to howl. Kalinka might have said that his howl was like a wolf's except that, having recently heard a wolf's howl, she recognized that a wolf's howl sounded much less plaintive than the dog's. Taras howled as if he was giving voice to some deep and enduring tragedy.

Kalinka put her arms around the dog's neck and hugged him close for comfort, but this did nothing to stop Taras from howling some more. He howled as if he held the sun itself responsible for a dreadful crime.

"What is it?" she said, stroking his long, fine head. "I wish I knew what it was that's upsetting you, boy."

Taras kept on howling. Kalinka had never seen an animal cry before, but she had the strong impression that she was looking at this now. The dog was crying as if his heart had been broken. There was something buried under the snow, perhaps, or in the wind, something terrible that Taras knew without seeing it for himself.

She'd heard of such things. An animal's sixth sense was what her father would have called it. And then, instinctively, Kalinka realized exactly what had happened, just as Taras had done several minutes before.

"It's Max, isn't it?" she whispered. "Something dreadful has happened to Max."

Taras barked an answer and then began to howl again, and this time Kalinka knew what Taras was doing: he was crying like a baby for his dead master. And she was certain that the dog's sixth sense could not have been wrong about something like that.

"Oh no," she breathed. "They wouldn't have. Surely. Not to that kind old man." But of course she knew perfectly well that the SS had murdered him, just as they had murdered her whole family and thousands of families like her own.

After what had happened in the botanical gardens at Monastyrsky Island, in Dnepropetrovsk, Kalinka had found no time to grieve for the deaths of her parents, her brothers and sisters, her grandparents and great-grandmother, her aunts and uncles and her cousins; the imperatives of her own unlikely survival and the sheer enormity of what had happened to her family—to everyone she knew—were almost too overwhelming. She felt sad for Max and for Taras—terribly sad—but, somehow, she still managed to hold her sadness in check. As always, she knew that if she started crying, she might never stop.

Kalinka sat down and started to pound the snow with her fists. "No! No! No!" she yelled at the sky. "After everything else, how could you let that happen?"

For a moment, she caught sight of herself as if from above, and she almost heard Max's voice inside her head.

"It's no good yelling at God," he would have said. "He had nothing to do with what happened. Don't blame him. Like you blamed him for what happened before. If you want to blame someone, young lady, then blame me for not getting you away from this place earlier. Blame the Germans for being stupid enough to elect Hitler, and invade Russia and Ukraine. Blame that stupid young captain for being such a fanatic. But don't go blaming old God."

Throughout all this, the two Przewalski's horses waited patiently for their companions to deal with their feelings; being wild animals, they were made of sterner stuff than the dog and the girl, and while they were capable of becoming depressed—Börte had lost a foal once and spent a whole summer pining for it—they were not creatures of emotion in the same way as a pet dog or an adolescent girl.

Temüjin allowed a decent interval to elapse before he nudged the girl in the back; it was time to get moving again. While his wild animal's senses had not registered the old man's death, they did now feel something else of vital importance. Sniffing the trail that they had left behind in the snow and placing his head close to the ground had alerted him to something that only an animal of a species that had been chased and killed by men for thousands of years until it was almost extinct could have felt in its bones.

They were being hunted.

CAPTAIN GRENZMANN BORROWED HIS sergeant's steel helmet and goggles, and had the man take the horse back to the stables at the big house while he took the sergeant's place in the sidecar of the BMW R75 motorcycle. Known as the Type Russia, the machine was more than equal to the task of riding across the snow-covered steppe at speed. During the invasion of Russia and Ukraine starting in June 1941, transport like this had enabled the German army to cover hundreds of kilometers in just a few days. So he was full of confidence about the success of their enterprise. Before they set off, however, he addressed the other three men, in order to impress upon them the importance of their mission.

"This won't take very long," he said. "We're after two wild Przewalski's horses and an escaped prisoner. I don't much care what happens to the dog, but the other three are the enemies of everything we've been fighting for since we came to the Soviet Union: a clean, open living space full of new beginnings and the past washed away for good. A place where we Germans can enjoy that which is our right. So we've no choice but to go after them. Now, they've left an obvious trail southeast of here, and it seems equally clear that they can't be traveling very quickly. It's not like these filthy horses can be ridden by anything except the lice and fleas they usually carry on their Gypsy backs. So they're walking. Which means we should catch up with them in just a few hours, well before we get anywhere near the Russian army lines."

The three SS men listened and nodded their approval but kept their thoughts to themselves; none of them dared to ask the captain the question that was on all of their minds: why were they wasting their time and effort going in pursuit of a couple of scruffy horses and a child? The size of the handprint on the wall of the water tank and the half-burned coat made that clear, at any rate. But as they took a closer look at the trail in the snow, another question presented itself to their already skeptical minds: just how was it possible that two wild Przewalski's horses, which had never been herded or domesticated in thousands of years, were willing to walk in a straight line behind a human being and a dog? Wild animals were wild animals, and none was wilder than those Przewalski's horses. Something as strange as that just didn't happen without a reason. It made no sense—at least none that could withstand rational explanation.

"Sir," said one of the men, a corporal called Hagen, "I'm not questioning your orders. But as you said yourself, that trail goes southeast, straight toward the Russian lines. Well, suppose the Russky lines are a lot nearer than we think they are? Isn't it possible that we might run straight into a Russian patrol before we catch up with these horses?"

The two other SS men nodded their agreement with what Hagen had found the courage to say.

Captain Grenzmann bit his lip and managed to contain his irritation; he disliked being questioned by his men, just as his own superiors in Berlin always disliked being questioned by a mere captain.

"I'm glad you've asked me that, Corporal Hagen," lied Grenzmann. "You make a good point. This is why I've asked the sergeant to return to the big house and to follow on with more troops and supplies. In case this takes a bit longer than I've anticipated. All right? All he has to do is follow our trail just as we are following that of these sub-equine horses."

"Yes, sir," said the corporal.

"But look here, the sooner we set off after them," said Grenzmann, "the sooner we'll catch up with them, and the sooner we can return to the big house and make plans to leave this awful place and go back to Germany. I promise you, men. This time tomorrow, it's northwest we'll be headed: toward our lines and the homeland."

Grenzmann neglected to mention that they would have to fight their way back to the German lines, of course, not that anyone was under any illusion about this; but anything was better than simply waiting for the Red Army to tighten its encirclement of Askaniya-Nova, and any mention of the word *homeland* was always guaranteed to bring smiles to everyone's faces. This was the positive news that they had all been waiting for. So it was with a renewed sense of optimism about their collective future that the Germans started the engines of their big motorcycles and set off after Kalinka and her unlikely trio of animal companions.

Seated in the sidecar of the lead motorcycle, Captain Grenzmann scanned the horizon eagerly with his sergeant's binoculars. He calculated that walking at a normal pace of six kilometers per hour, their quarry couldn't have traveled more than thirty kilometers; even with a sidecar and a heavy machine gun, the Type Russia motorcycle could easily cover that kind of distance in an hour or two. With any luck, they could deal with the child and the horses, and be back at the big house in time for a celebratory dinner of horse meat.

Finally, they seemed to be nearing the end of the flat and featureless steppe. Ahead of them, they could see some hills and a few trees and the possibility of shelter from the unforgiving, icy wind.

"At least we're going to have somewhere to hide if they catch up with us now," said Kalinka.

Taras barked and ran off to scout the way ahead, as was now his habit: he would race away like a bolt of lightning and then return a few minutes later, wagging his tail and grinning if he thought everything looked safe.

Kalinka pulled gently on Börte's makeshift bridle. "Whoa, there," she said. "While Taras is gone, I think I should take a bearing. Just to check we're headed in the right direction."

She jumped down off the horse, stretched her legs for a moment and put her hand in her coat pocket to find the compass, but to her alarm, it wasn't there.

"I can't have lost our compass," she said, checking the other pocket of the Astrakhan coat. "Can I?" But there was no sign of it in the other pocket either.

"I have lost it," she muttered. "How could I be so stupid?"

Temüjin snorted with what sounded like irritation.

Kalinka shook her head. "I haven't taken a bearing—well, since I mounted Börte. I guess it must have fallen out of my pocket when I jumped up on your back."

Börte flicked her furry tail as if there was nothing to be done about it now. Kalinka ran her hand along the mare's short mane with affection; against her palm, it felt oddly comforting. Börte seemed to like it, too.

Kalinka looked back at the trail. In spite of the sun's now setting to one side of them—its warmth had melted only a little of the snow—their trail was still clearly visible. But there could be no possibility of retracing their steps to look for the compass. That was just asking for trouble.

Fortunately, she had not lost the bread and the cheese and the money Max had given her, which amounted to ten karbovanets and six rubles, but of course none of this was going to help them travel in the right direction. "Max said that I could always navigate by the sun—which sets in the west, so I suppose east is that way." She pointed to their left. "And with the trail behind us, from what I imagine must be the northwest, I calculate the southeasterly direction must be this one."

Kalinka nodded ahead of them, in roughly the same direction from whence even now Taras was returning. He came toward her, licked her hand and wagged his tail, which everyone found reassuring. Even Temüjin, who wagged his tail back at the dog.

It seemed like the proper moment to eat. Kalinka would have shared the bread and cheese with the horses but for the fact that she knew they weren't supposed to eat bread or cheese—it wasn't good for them. But she gave some of the cheese to Taras, which he appeared to enjoy, so she assumed it was good for him. Some crows appeared as if from nowhere and set about collecting the few crumbs that she and the wolfhound dropped onto the ground. Life was hard for everyone on the steppe in winter, even crows.

While Kalinka and the dog—and the crows—consumed the food Max had given them, they helped the horses clear snow from some grass so that they could eat, too. But Temüjin's mind was not on his stomach; he kept lifting his shoe box–sized head and looking back the way they had come, as if searching for a glimpse of their pursuers.

Kalinka could tell he was anxious about it, which seemed to suggest that the SS were getting closer.

"How far behind do you think they are, Temüjin?" she asked him.

Temüjin shook his head.

"Motorcycles?"

The horse nodded.

"How many?"

He tapped his hoof on the ground twice.

"Not that it really matters how many, since they have guns. We might just outrun a German on a motorcycle, but we can't outrun their bullets."

She thought for a moment. "You know, if we do catch sight of them, then it might make sense for us all to scatter in four directions. There's no way they can come after us all. And once we get to those trees, they might easily lose one of us, or more."

This made sense, of course, although to the three animals, it seemed pointless answering her until necessity demanded it. Taras had already concluded he would defend the girl to the death, as he was certain Max had already done; the throat of a man seated in a motorcycle sidecar would be easy to catch in his powerful jaws. It would be a sweet and perhaps even tasty revenge.

"Especially once it starts to get dark," she added. "Which won't be long now." She glanced up at the sky. "I just realized. We've been walking all day. Max would be proud of us, don't you think? That we managed to get this far."

Taras barked his agreement.

Kalinka waited for Börte to stop eating cold grass and then mounted her again.

They set off along the track that Taras had already made, and before long they were over the brow of a strange-looking hill that was studded with a circle of odd standing stones, which had been there since the beginning of civilization and looked like rotten, jagged teeth sticking out of the gums of the ground. The stones were marked with curious designs that must have signified something to the people who made them but meant nothing to Kalinka. Her father had been a very smart man, but she figured even he couldn't have told her what the designs were supposed to represent.

"What was it he used to tell us?" she murmured as they walked through the stone circle. " 'The older I get, the less I know.' " She shook her head. "I never knew what that meant until now. I guess it just means that there's so much in the world we can't hope to understand but that it's all right not to understand it, just as long as you realize that no one could hope to understand everything. I know I don't. But frankly, the older I get, the less I even care."

At the bottom of the hill was a thick line of conifer trees, where the wolfhound ate a large pinecone and the horses nibbled at some tree bark, which they seemed to enjoy; in just a few minutes, they each managed to chew a complete ring around two trunks, and Kalinka didn't have the heart to point out that this only made their trail easier to follow. Even if it was dark by the time the Germans reached this place. Not that she thought Grenzmann and his men were going to slow down much when it got dark: as well as large-caliber machine guns, the sidecars on their motorcycles were equipped with powerful searchlights.

Kalinka and the animals resumed their journey at a trot and passed quickly through tall silver birch trees and around another hill. They made what seemed like good progress for thirty minutes or more until they came upon another clump of pine trees, but there an uncomfortable discovery awaited them: they were looking at the same two pine trees from which the horses had eaten the bark earlier on.

Kalinka almost fell off Börte's back with disappointment.

"Oh no," she sighed wearily. "We've come in a complete circle. We're back where we were a while ago. Look. The stone circle we passed through is at the top of that hill. Well, so much for my navigation." She shook her head. "It's all my fault. You make mistakes when you're tired. But I promise I won't let it happen again."

They came to a halt while Kalinka decided what to do. Given the fact that Temüjin was now distinctly nervous— his whole body was atremble, as if he sensed the Germans were much closer now—this setback seemed disastrous; but above all she sensed the importance of not panicking. Their very survival depended on it.

"Wait a minute." She glanced up at the darkening sky and thought for a moment. "What do I know about the stars?" she asked herself. "Maybe I can figure out the best way to go from them. Isn't that how people used to get around in the old days? Before compasses were invented? When they used that stone circle for telling them important stuff about the seasons, probably. And maybe which way is southeast."

Kalinka turned the mare slowly and searched the heavens until she found what she was looking for.

"There. The seven stars that make up the Saucepan. And that's Cassiopeia, which is always on the opposite side of . . . yes, there it is: the North Star. That sits right over the North Pole, and unlike the other stars, it does not appear to move. So as long as we know that, then we know this direction must be south."

Taras yawned an infectious yawn that Kalinka found impossible not to copy. She'd never felt as tired as this before—not even when she'd run away from the botanical gardens in Dnepropetrovsk and hid in a closet for several weeks—but sleep was now her enemy. If they stopped and rested now, they'd surely be caught and killed.

"We'd better get going!" she yelled at the others. "There's no time to waste. With any luck, we can make up some of the time we've lost."

She banged her thighs against Börte's rough flanks, and the mare broke into a gallop.

"It's this way. I'm certain of it."

T HINGS WENT WRONG FOR Captain Grenzmann and his men soon after they set off in pursuit of Kalinka and the horses.

First, one of the BMW motorcycles suffered a flat tire, which meant a delay of almost an hour while Corporal Hagen carried out the repair; fortunately for the SS, there was a spare wheel on the back of each sidecar. Then, almost as soon as they set off again, the other motorcycle collided with a rock that was buried in the snow, and the rider bruised his chest against the outsized fuel tank, while Captain Grenzmann broke a tooth and cut his lip on the handle of the machine gun. The collision buckled the motorcycle's front wheel, and they were obliged to change that one, too. The accident shook them up; it made them realize that the apparently featureless steppe was actually full of unpleasant surprises, and that not all of them were the Red Army.

The discovery close to the trail of a dead wolf was another surprise, and Grenzmann's men were discomfited by Corporal Hagen's suggestion that the wolf might have been killed by the horses and the dog acting as a team.

"It's just like the Bremen Town musicians," he said. "In the Brothers Grimm story."

"I never heard such rubbish," said Grenzmann. "It was just instinct, that's all. The wolf attacked and they all reacted. Simple as that."

In spite of the strengthening sun, the trail in the snow remained clear—clear enough to provide further discouragement for Grenzmann's men, because after a while, they noticed that the child was no longer walking but riding, and riding a wild horse at that, which did not, they considered, bode well for their enterprise. They'd all seen the Przewalski's horses at Askaniya-Nova and considered them wilder than most wild horses; they knew how aggressive and untamable they could be, and how fast—perhaps as fast on snow as a motorcycle. A few of the SS men had even come to admire the strong spirit of these horses with the same grudging respect they held for the Red Army.

"I never heard of a wild horse that would let someone ride it, just like that," said Corporal Hagen. "Or one that would protect a child against a wolf. It just doesn't make sense. From what little I know about horses, it can take months to tame one."

"Can't be done," said the man seated in the corporal's

sidecar; his name was Donkels. "Not unless that someone was very special."

"What do you know about horses?" sneered the captain.

"It's weird, that's what it is, sir," insisted Hagen. "Uncanny. Most wild horses would kill themselves trying to throw someone off their backs. Or give you a pretty savage bite. Maybe even trample you to death. Like they trampled that wolf. And yet this child climbs up on one, just like that. As if it was the most natural thing in the world. Doesn't make sense."

"What do we know about this child anyway?" shouted the man driving the lead motorcycle. He had to shout because of the noise of the engine.

"We know all that we need to know," said the captain from his sidecar. "As SS, we know all that's important to know. And we know our duty, so let that be enough for you." And he squeezed the trigger on the sidecar-mounted machine gun, letting off a few rounds at some crows just to show his men that he meant business.

The corporal nodded, but his sense that this was a mission doomed from the outset was not diminished by the captain's smooth words, nor was anyone else's sense of the same. And as the morning gave way to afternoon and still they had not caught up with their quarry, all of the men except the captain began to doubt the wisdom of going any farther. Now, soldiers are often superstitious people, and in spite of the young captain's assurances, the three had started to arrive at the same conclusion: that the refugee child who had painted the strange pictures on the walls of the disused water tank had established a mysterious bond with the wild horses, of the kind that they'd all encountered in the myths and legends they'd read as boys. Hadn't the great German hero Siegfried owned an almost magical steed whom no one had ever mounted, called Grani, sired from Sleipnir, who belonged to Odin himself and whom the god Baldr had ridden for nine long nights into Hel? Wasn't it possible that these wild Przewalski's horses were just a little bit like Grani and Sleipnir? And given that all of the SS soldiers had eaten the meat of these same horses, weren't they courting disaster by going after their blood brother and sister?

When they stopped to refuel from the big jerry cans they were carrying and to eat their horse-meat sandwiches, Corporal Hagen was appointed to express their doubts to Captain Grenzmann and to suggest, strongly, that they turn back.

"If we go much farther, then we won't have enough fuel to get back to the big house," said the corporal. "Not to mention the fact that we'll have to spend the night out here, on the steppe, in the freezing cold, without tents, without a hot dinner. And don't forget that there are wolves about. And Red Army soldiers, perhaps."

"Then it's very fortunate that we have machine guns," said Captain Grenzmann. "Besides, I told the sergeant to follow us with more supplies, didn't I? So we're doubly fortunate."

His men finished refueling the motorcycles and resumed the chase in a sulk that became so profound that, after a while, Captain Grenzmann felt obliged to lift their spirits with a song. They sang "Erika," which is a song about a flower that grows in Germany; it was also a favorite marching song for the German army. But with only four of them singing and without a military band, it didn't sound the same.

They gave up singing when they came across the circle of standing stones on top of a hill; in the twilight, it was an eerie place, and they half expected to see some wicked giants and perhaps a few Rhine maidens, or their Ukrainian equivalents.

"I don't like this place," said Hagen.

"Me neither," said Donkels. "It gives me a peculiar feeling, as if we're not supposed to be here. As if this whole business was jinxed from the outset."

"That's enough," said Grenzmann, but he, too, was touched by the peculiar atmosphere of the circle and a feeling that things had not gone entirely to plan; at that point, he might have ordered them to turn back but for the fact that he didn't want to lose face in front of his men.

Optimism that their quest might be coming to an end was restored at the bottom of the slope with the discovery of the pine trees with the rings of missing bark.

"These trees were chewed by horses," explained Grenzmann. He sounded triumphant and perhaps a little mad. "For the minerals. Horses do that sometimes. And what's more, these trees were chewed recently, too. D'you see? The girdles of the trees are still sticky."

He climbed stiffly out of the sidecar to inspect some horse dung on the ground. It was still moist to the touch.

"And this dung is fresh. So they can't be far away from us now. I can feel it. They're close. Very close. It's only a question of finding them."

IN THE ARCHING LIGHT of a big white Ukrainian moon, Kalinka picked a circuitous, winding route through the silver trees in order to make it difficult for the motorized Germans to follow them, but in the deeper snow of the forest, progress was painfully slow. Börte was carrying her head below shoulder level, and even Temüjin had stopped flicking his furry tail; every so often, he would nuzzle the mare's neck with encouraging snorts and nibbles because she was very tired. Kalinka herself was slumped on her forearms against Börte's neck, as if she still had some boring schoolwork to complete before going to bed. Only Taras seemed to have energy; he had gone ahead on one of his regular reconnaissance missions. Somehow he always knew where to come and find Kalinka and the two Przewalski's.

"We'll find somewhere to rest soon," she told Börte. "We have to."

Temüjin stopped and listened for a moment and looked at Kalinka, wondering if she could hear what he could hear.

"What is it?" she asked him as Börte came to a halt beside the stallion's muscular flank. "Can you hear something? Me, I can't hear anything."

His own question answered, Temüjin paced the snow impatiently and then bit Börte on the shoulder; the mare's head jerked up. Now he had her full attention, and immediately he set off at a canter, with the mare following and Kalinka just holding on to the belt around Börte's neck.

A couple of minutes later, the girl heard the engines of the German motorcycles, and even though she was already freezing cold, she felt an extra chill down her back.

"What are we going to do?" she said.

But Temüjin knew, even if the girl did not. Ahead of them was a big conifer tree; he paused for a moment, looked around to see that Börte was behind him and then pushed his way through the lowest snow-covered branches.

Kalinka squealed and pressed her head into Börte's neck as snow tumbled onto the mare's back and down the collar of the girl's coat. She was about to complain when she realized that Temüjin had cleverly led them to a dark area under a thick canopy of branches, where the ground was dry and they were almost completely hidden from view. It was immediately obvious that this was the kind of ingenious natural hiding place that the Przewalski's horses had used before.

Taras was with them again, full of alarm at the nearness of the Germans; but recognizing the need for complete silence, he managed to contain his agitation and lay down right away on a deep bed of pine needles. Kalinka jumped off Börte's back and did the same, hugging the wolfhound close for security and warmth. The dog began to chew a pinecone quietly and quite enjoyed it.

"Won't they see our tracks?" whispered Kalinka.

Temüjin had already considered this possibility; the stallion crept stealthily across the diameter of their hiding place to the other side of the tree trunk, squeezed through the branches there and galloped off. Kalinka guessed that he had gone to lay a false trail for the Germans.

"He's such a clever horse," she told Börte.

Meanwhile, the mare knelt down, tucked her legs underneath her rear and closed her tired brown eyes.

Minutes passed, and the sound of the BMW motorcycles grew closer as they labored noisily through the snow. Kalinka could see their headlights now and hear German-speaking voices. She could smell the exhaust fumes from their machines; in the clear, fresh air, she could even smell the tobacco in their cigarettes and the sausage on their breaths. Her heart was in her mouth, but she still found time to wonder that any motorcycle could make it across such difficult ground, let alone one with a sidecar; she wasn't to know that the Type Russia machine had three-wheel drive when it was combined with a sidecar, which made it highly maneuverable.

"The trail stops here," said a voice. "At this big tree. It's just as if they disappeared."

"You idiot," said another man. "Of course they haven't disappeared. This isn't some fairy story, you know. I never met such an impressionable, superstitious bunch as you men. Really, you astonish me sometimes."

The Germans had stopped right beside their hiding place; they had kept their engines running and appeared to be studying the trail. One of them had climbed off his machine and was walking around the tree.

Suddenly Kalinka had an overwhelming desire to sneeze, so she pinched her nose, held her breath, closed her eyes and prayed that the Germans would not find them.

"The trail resumes on the other side, Captain," said the German who'd circled the tree. "They must have gone under this conifer and sneaked out the other side in an effort to throw us off their trail. Smart idea. Do you suppose it was the child who thought of that or the horses?"

"These Przewalski's are known for their cunning," said another voice. "They may look like horses, but the fact is they're not really proper horses at all but more of a counter-race of Gypsy horses: an inbred mixture of species that should have died out years ago. Biologically speaking, they're duds. Like the dodo. But they still exhibit strong and primitive instincts for survival, and to that extent, they're more like rats than horses. Which probably accounts for their cunning. And explains why

185

Berlin wants them eliminated. To that extent, they and the person traveling with them have much in common. Come on. We'll pick up the trail on the other side. Won't be long until we have them now. I'm sure of it."

The motorcycles started to rev up again and then drove around the tree to the place from where Temüjin had begun the false trail.

Kalinka let out her breath and hugged Taras, who licked her face with relief.

"They're gone, I think."

Taras crawled to the edge of the canopy and peered out, then came back with his tail wagging.

"That was too close for comfort," said Kalinka.

Taras let his lip curl; being near to a German sounded good to him just as long as he could bite one.

"Now all we have to do is wait for Temüjin to come and find us again," Kalinka told him.

Taras barked.

The girl shrugged and looked around. "At least we're dry. And it's out of the wind."

Once again, Kalinka was too alert to sleep. She thrust her frozen hands into the pockets of her Astrakhan coat, and felt the money that Max had given her. Suddenly she remembered him telling her he'd given her something to remember him by, and since there was nothing else in her pockets but matches, she took out the money. Between two greasy banknotes, she found a folded piece of notepaper. It was too dark under the tree to read it, so she struck a match and saw that there was writing on the paper.

"Max wrote me a letter!" she told Taras. "How wonderful."

Tara sniffed the letter, caught a strong scent of his master's hands and whined.

"Would you like to hear it? Of course you would."

Kalinka struck a second match and started to read:

"My dear Kalinka,

"It's been a very long time since I wrote a letter—so long that I have almost forgotten how— and I wish I had more time to write this one. As I think I told you, I never had any children of my own, but if I had, I certainly couldn't have wished for a better daughter than you. Somewhere, your own father and mother are very proud. You are a great credit to them.

"I haven't known you for very long, but you are a remarkable young lady and you have my admiration, not just for your having survived the terrible events in Dnepropetrovsk, but also because in all my years I never knew anyone who could win the trust of these Przewalski's horses. I envy you that and wonder if you can explain it yourself.

"Anyway, that was one of the things I wanted to tell you. I remembered you called them tarpan

horses. That was incorrect. I wanted to remind
you that these are not tarpan horses. Tarpan
horses were gray, and had manes that hung down
on one side, and forelocks; they were also smaller
than the Przewalski's horse. I say were *because*
tarpan are certainly extinct; the last one died—
poor thing—in 1918, in captivity at Poltava."

Kalinka shook out the match and lit another to finish
reading her letter.

"The same thing must not be allowed to hap-
pen to these Przewalski's; one of the things that
makes living in this world so wonderful is the fan-
tastic variety of all the races and species that are
in it, and it would be a crime to let the same thing
happen to the Przewalski's as has happened to so
many other species of animal. But I am convinced
that if anyone can save them, it's you. Don't let
me down, Kalinka; more importantly, don't let
the Przewalski's horses down. You must get them
to a place of safety.

"You have already suffered great hardship,
and in the days ahead, there may come even more
despair; so I also wanted to tell you about a great
Russian grand master of chess—as perhaps you
yourself will be one day—called Savielly Tarta-
kower. In 1911, his parents were murdered, just

like yours, and in very similar circumstances; but by 1935, he was one of the main organizers of the Chess Olympiad in Warsaw. Tartakower was almost as well known for his great wisdom as for playing chess, and I had to write down a few of the clever things he said that may help you in the coming days and years. They are about chess, but in a way, they are also about life. Here they are, in no particular order:

"'It's always better to sacrifice your opponent's men.'

"'The mistakes are all there on the board, just waiting to be made.'

"' The move is there, but you must see it.'

"'Chess is a fairy tale of 1,001 blunders.'

"And my own favorite: 'Moral victories do not count.'

"I am not a wise man like Tartakower. But one important thing I have learned is that nothing good ever comes of hate. It would be all too easy and understandable for you to hate the Germans for what they did to your family. But please try always to remember that it was a German— the baron Falz-Fein—who created the sanctuary at Askaniya-Nova, and there was a time when I thought that this particular German was the most wonderful man in the world. I promise you that there will certainly be other good Germans like

him. I hope that one day you get a chance to meet a German such as he was.

"Good luck to you all. I know you will need it. But with God's grace, I know you can come through this ordeal.

"Your affectionate friend,
Maxim Borisovich Melnik

"PS. Stroke Taras for me."

Kalinka blew out the third match and stroked Taras as Max had told her; then she laid her head against the tree and closed her eyes for just a moment and wished that she could have hugged the old man and thanked him again for his kindness.

"When you think about it," she told Taras, "it's not such a bad world that has men in it like Maxim Borisovich Melnik."

TEMÜJIN WAS GONE FOR less than an hour, but to those who slept under the heavy boughs of the big conifer tree, it seemed much longer. Laying a false trail in the snow to deceive the Germans had been the work of only ten or fifteen minutes, and most of the remaining time he had spent looking for a warmer place for Kalinka, Börte and Taras to hide—a woodsman's hut or perhaps an old barn—as the stallion was certain they could go no farther without sleep. The dog, he was sure, was like him and could have run forever, for that is characteristic of the borzoi breed, but the girl was exhausted, and Börte— who was the focus of Temüjin's extra concern—almost as tired.

After a while, he sensed that there was a much better hiding place close by. He could not explain how he knew this, but it was as if his ancestors had called out to him from hundreds—perhaps thousands—of years ago; and suddenly his nose seemed to tell him which way to go.

Kalinka awoke with a start to find the sleeve of her coat in the stallion's mouth and that she was being tugged urgently to her feet. Taras and Börte were already standing, ready to leave the cover of the tree canopy.

"What is it?" she asked sleepily. "Why did you wake me? Are the Germans coming back?"

Temüjin stamped his foot.

"I can't hear anything," she said. "Couldn't we stay under here, where it's dry and out of the wind? I never thought I'd say it, but really, it's quite comfortable sleeping on needles."

Temüjin stamped his foot again, only this time with real impatience.

"It's just that I'm tired. So very tired. I think I could sleep for a hundred years."

Kalinka leaned across Börte's back for a moment and closed her eyes, and this time, Temüjin dropped his head and bit her on the thigh.

"Ow," she said, rubbing her leg. "That really hurt. What's the big idea? I thought we were supposed to be friends, Temüjin."

The stallion swung his head around and walked away; then he turned to see if Kalinka was following.

"All right, all right," she said. "You want us to leave this place. I understand that. Although it beats me why."

As Temüjin led the way out from under the tree, a

branch sprang back and dumped a large deposit of snow on Kalinka's head; hearing the girl yelp with surprise and discomfort, he looked back and laughed, certain that she was properly awake now. He needed her full attention to reach the sanctuary that, in his bones, he knew to be close at hand.

Kalinka wiped the snow from her hair and off her face without further complaint and mounted Börte. To her surprise, the stallion began to lead them back the way they had come earlier.

"I get it," she murmured. "We're doubling back on our own trail. Good idea. That should confuse the Germans. It will be harder for them to track us now. You're so clever, Temüjin. I'd never have thought of doing something like that."

Temüjin broke into a trot and Börte followed. Soon they were running past the same trees where the horses had chewed off the bark and up the hill toward the circle of standing stones. Here the stallion paused and then walked off at a tangent toward an inner group of central stones, and it was only now that Kalinka perceived a pattern in the arrangement of the circle: all of the stones were positioned in an elliptical spiral with a clearly identifiable middle point where the stones appeared to become shorter. As they reached this middle point, she realized that it was not that the stones were shorter at all—that was only an illusion—but that the ground was much lower here, and the stones led the way down a cleverly disguised pathway into a deep depression in the hill. From the back of the mare, Kalinka saw how you might have walked straight past this central spiral of stones and never realized that it seemed to lead to a place that must have been of great importance to the ancient people who had built it.

At the bottom of the spiral path, Temüjin stopped and looked around.

"Yes, it's certainly interesting," said Kalinka. "All right, we can't be seen down here, but we're still outside, in the freezing cold, and I don't understand how we're better off here than we were under that tree."

Temüjin was already digging in the snow with his hoof, which prompted Taras to start digging. Finally Kalinka jumped off Börte's back, and ignoring the cold in her hands, she began digging, too.

"If this is buried treasure we're digging for," she said, "I'm not sure how that's going to help us. Although I suppose we could always try to bribe the Germans to let us go."

A couple of times, she had to stop and warm her numb hands underneath her arms.

At last, Temüjin's hoof struck something hard, and the next second, the remaining snow collapsed to reveal two large standing stones with a stone beam across the top.

"It's an entrance to something," said Kalinka. "But how did you know it was here, Temüjin?"

The stallion snorted and then sniffed at the length and

breadth of a wooden door as if something lay behind it. The design carved on the door was the same as the one on the stones; and now that Kalinka took a closer look, she could just about make out what it was.

"Why, it's a horse," she said. "Of course. Why didn't I realize that before? It's an ancient horse like you, Temüjin."

Temüjin tossed his head up and down, anxious now that the girl should open the door.

"You can smell something in there, is that it?"

Temüjin nodded, and marked time for a moment like a horse in a dressage competition. Taras barked.

"You too, huh?"

Kalinka pushed hard, but the door did not move. She smacked it with frustration; the door didn't sound as if it was very thick, but moving it was beyond her.

"It's no good," she said finally. "I can't shift it. Not that I really expected I could. This door looks like it's been here for thousands of years. I mean, well done for finding it, but I really don't see that we've achieved anything."

Temüjin sighed with frustration and turned away from the door with what Kalinka thought looked like disgust. The next second, he lashed out at the door with his powerful hind legs.

Thinking she was witnessing an outburst of equine temper, Kalinka walked quickly up the slope and out of the way. Taras yelped and followed with his tail between his long legs. Both of them still remembered the savage kick Temüjin had delivered to the wolf; the poor animal must have flown six or seven meters through the air.

"Hey, take it easy, Temüjin. There's no need to get angry about this."

But Temüjin wasn't angry. He was only doing what clearly needed to be done—he was kicking in the door. Börte turned and helped him with her own back hooves, and within a matter of a few minutes, the two Przewalski's horses had reduced the ancient door to matchwood.

Temüjin breathed a sigh of relief as the girl stepped inside, struck a match and put the tiny flame to a small stone censer that was mounted on the wall behind the demolished door; finally it seemed she was good for something after all: fire and light.

A strong smell of burning animal fat filled the air, and the entrance lit up to reveal a wide, curving passage that was a continuation of the spiral design they had seen on the ground outside.

Kalinka lifted the censer off a hook on the wall and led the way down into the shadows. Her teeth were chattering, but not just with cold—she was afraid. There was something about the place that reminded her of the crypt in Nikopol, where she had spent a very disagreeable week.

"I wouldn't do this if I wasn't frozen to the marrow," she admitted. "I don't think I could ever be an archaeologist and go inside some dead pharaoh's pyramid."

After several minutes, the passage opened up to reveal

a much larger space. Kalinka found another censer and lit it, and then another, and before long, she saw that they were in an ancient burial chamber. The high, vaulted ceiling was covered with paintings—cave paintings of horses and a young woman wearing long robes, who appeared to wield power over them and some kneeling tribesmen. On the floor was a sword. Kalinka picked it up and looked at the old weapon in the flickering lamplight and scraped the edge with her thumb: the blade was still very sharp.

"It's made of bronze," she said. "I don't know how old that makes this place exactly, but from the look of those people painted on the ceiling, I'll bet we're the first people in here in at least two or three thousand years."

Temüjin and Börte were sniffing at the skeletons of many dead animals that lay in a huge circle on the stone floor. The skeletons were dressed in ancient harnesses and armor, and it took Kalinka a moment or two to see that these were all skeletons of ancient horses, and that most of the skeletons showed signs of having met violent deaths.

"I'm beginning to understand how you found this place," she said to Temüjin. "You could smell them, couldn't you? And no wonder—there must be at least fifty dead horses in here. Perhaps more." She glanced at the sword. "And I'll bet this is the sword that they were killed with."

Out of respect for Temüjin and Börte, she put the sword down—just in case it made them feel nervous.

"But why? Why would anyone kill all these horses and bury them?"

The answer to her question was soon revealed, for in the center of this circle of horse skeletons, holding a bronze spear and wearing a helmet and breastplate, was the mummified corpse of a girl not much older than Kalinka herself. Kalinka guessed she was probably the same girl depicted on the ceiling painting.

"A warrior princess. That's what she must have been. Or perhaps a priestess. That would certainly explain why those tribesmen are kneeling in front of her in the pictures on the ceiling. I guess they must have slaughtered all of these poor horses when she died: so that they could serve her in the next life. The same way they used to bury a pharaoh with all his possessions."

Feeling sorry for her, Kalinka laid a kind hand on the mummified girl's breastplate.

"I think she must have been very beautiful," she whispered. "I wonder what happened to her. It makes you think, doesn't it, Taras? That you're not the only girl with problems in this world. I mean, look at her. Did she just die of some illness, perhaps? Or was she killed, like her horses? In battle by her enemies? I don't suppose we shall ever know for sure what happened to her, but I should like to have known her."

Kalinka bowed her head in respect for the little warrior priestess for a moment.

"Dear lady, you are not forgotten," she said quietly.

Temüjin and Börte were still sniffing at the skeletons, as if they wanted to make quite sure that they were dead.

"I'm sorry," Kalinka said to them. "This must be very upsetting for you both. To see so many of your kind in a mass grave like this. I'd like to apologize to you on behalf of humankind, in general. I may be just a child with little experience of the world, but it seems that people are capable of great cruelty, not just to animals but also to each other. You hear all sorts of terrible stories these days. I even heard tell of people in the south who were so hungry, they ate their own children. Max is right; I don't think it does any good to hate. But you can't help feeling more than a little disappointed now and again that man is such a destructive species. I don't suppose the priestess would have allowed them to do such a terrible thing as kill all these horses if she'd been alive. I know I would certainly have forbidden it."

Taras barked and sat down. The ancient burial chamber made him feel uneasy—he sensed that there were ancient forces at work in the ancient tomb, and he thought there could be little chance of sleeping comfortably in such a place. But for the moment, there seemed to be no other place that they could go.

"I hope she won't mind us disturbing her grave like this," said Kalinka. "Then again, what can she do?"

Taras barked and let the bark turn into a sort of whine—he sensed that there was a lot more the dead warrior priestess could have done about their presence there than evidently Kalinka suspected, and already he half expected to see or feel a ghost. Max might not have believed in ghosts and spirits, but like most dogs, Taras was much less skeptical about such things. Besides, there was a lot more to being a spirit than appearing in the form of an apparition or going bump in the night. Spirits could affect what people did, and sometimes they could even take them over. How else could you explain someone like Captain Grenzmann, who was possessed with the idea of his own countrymen's superiority over all other peoples?

Kalinka had wandered off with one of the lamps to explore.

"There's everything here that you could want if you were a warrior priestess," she said. "Armor, weapons, even a chariot—all perfectly preserved. Who knows? Perhaps she could have helped us fight the Germans. I wouldn't be at all surprised if she could have defeated them, too. I mean, just look at the blades on the wheels of this chariot. And her bow and arrows on the side of the platform. I'll bet she was pretty formidable in her day. I'm sure some of those jars must contain food and drink, although I'm not going to risk it—not after all this time. Even though I'm very hungry."

She opened one of the jars anyway and put her fingers inside it experimentally.

"Actually, it's not food in this jar," she said. "It seems to be what looks like a sort of paint. Silver paint. I could have used some of this back at Askaniya-Nova. For the walls of our cave. I might have painted some silver horses. What do you think about that, Taras?"

Taras yawned. All of a sudden, he felt as if he could sleep after all; was there something in that strange-smelling animal fat burning in the censer that was making him feel as if he could not stay awake a minute longer? Or was it just the sense that they were safe after all—at least for a while?

Börte lay down with a sigh and closed her eyes. Temüjin went to inspect the chariot, but only as a way of staving off tiredness. He, too, wanted to lie down and sleep.

"Well, I don't know about all of you," said Kalinka, "but I am going to get some sleep. Let's hope that the Germans don't find this place. I don't suppose there's any way out of here other than the way we came in."

Kalinka lay down next to Börte and laid an arm across the horse's neck as if the animal were a teddy bear; she told herself that a living, breathing horse was much more comforting to sleep with than some smelly old stuffed toy.

Temüjin lay down beside the old chariot; he flicked his furry tail a couple of times and closed his dark eyes. He could not explain why he trusted the girl and believed at the core of his being that she could help save his species, any more than he could account for how he had known that the ancient stone circle should have concealed a place of holy sanctuary for them; but he did and he had, and that was all the reason that was needed for a creature such as him. He liked the girl even more for what she had said about her own kind.

The last to sleep was Taras. The wolfhound yawned and lay down beside the girl; strangely, all of his previous worries about the place were now gone. His companions were out of the cold bora wind, and that was all that seemed important.

He dreamed a vivid dream of ancient tribesmen and their young warrior priestess, of her horses and of the wicked Germans.

CORPORAL HAGEN CLIMBED OFF his motorcycle, walked stiffly across the snow to the end of the trail and shook his head.

"The tracks stop dead right here, sir," he said. "It looks as though they doubled back on their own trail, which means we must have driven straight past them somewhere. Probably in those woods." Hagen took off his steel helmet and rubbed his squarish head for a moment. His leather coat creaked as his arm moved, and it sounded just like the snow shifting under his boots as he walked. "You did say this was a child we were after, sir, didn't you?"

"You know I did," said Captain Grenzmann. "Why do you ask?"

"Only it's not many children who could lay a false trail like this and would have the nerve to hide from us as we passed straight by them."

"S'right, sir," said the SS man called Donkels. "This can't be any ordinary child."

"Unless it was the horses that did it," said the third SS man. "Them being as cunning as you said they were."

"That would be very cunning for a horse," said Donkels. "A horse would have to be as cunning as a fox to do something like that."

"And I keep telling you that's exactly what these horses are like," insisted Grenzmann.

"Well," said Hagen, "it seems we have to go back the same way we came." He yawned, wiped the inside of his helmet with a handkerchief and then placed it back on his head. "Look, sir. Why don't we call it a day? Or more accurately, a night, since that's what this is. We've been on their trail now for what—eighteen hours? We tried our best to catch them and we've failed. Not that anyone ever needs to know that, sir."

"I will know it, Corporal," Grenzmann said coldly.

"All I'm saying, sir, is that since we are now returning the way we came, why don't we keep going until we run into the sergeant and the rest of our men? Perhaps they've made camp back there. We can rest up a bit, get some hot food inside us and then try again tomorrow." He shrugged. "Who knows? Maybe we'll see some sign of the horses when it's light. But if we don't then, where's the harm in just going back to the big house at Askaniya-Nova? A couple of wild horses and a child. I mean, really, sir, is it worth all this effort?"

"That's right, sir," said Donkels. "No one could have done more than you did. Anyone else but you would have given up ages ago."

"You think so, huh?"

"Yes, sir. You've been quite relentless, sir."

"But now the time has come to give up, is that what you're saying?"

"Yes, sir."

"Let me tell you what I think about that idea."

Grenzmann drew his pistol, laid it on his lap and stared at it meaningfully. The other three men shifted awkwardly.

"We're going on with the search," Grenzmann said firmly. "Until we find them. Do you understand? Nobody is going to quit now. Need I remind you that this is a breeding pair of Przewalski's horses we're pursuing and we have a duty to cleanse the earth of their wandering kind forever? That's a duty I'm not about to shirk just because you are all feeling tired. And anyone who wants to argue about this can take it up with Mr. Luger here." Grenzmann paused. "Anyone? How about you, Corporal?"

Hagen shook his head.

"No, I thought not. So let's have a little less argument and a little more enthusiasm. Now mount that motorcycle, Corporal, and let's move, shall we? There's no time to waste. As you say, it's clear they've doubled back. That can only mean that they know we're close to catching them. In spite of what you say, we haven't failed yet. Not by a long way."

Hagen saluted smartly and climbed onto his motorcycle; he had no love for Grenzmann, but he feared the captain and he knew the others feared him, too. It was fear that kept them all in line and often made them obey orders they sometimes found distasteful; at least that was what they had told themselves.

Minutes later, they were speeding back along the frozen trail.

An hour's hard ride brought them back to the circle of standing stones, and they might have carried straight on because the previous tracks of their own wheels were much more noticeable in the moonlight than anything else. The ancient monument was almost behind them when Grenzmann glanced back over his shoulder and noticed two lines of hoofprints leading off at a tangent and over the brow of the hill. He slapped the arm of the man beside him and pointed.

"There's the trail," he said. "Get in front of the corporal's machine and make him follow you."

The BMW sped quickly ahead, and taking over the lead, Grenzmann's rider turned the small pursuit party back up the hill and toward the center of the stone circle. When they arrived there, Grenzmann saw that the tracks went down one side of the dip but did not come up again.

"What did I tell you?"

Grinning broadly, he held up his hand and brought the pursuit party to a halt.

"They must be hiding down there," he said. "Turn off your engines and dismount. We'll go the rest of the way on foot. Better bring a flashlight, Corporal."

With machine pistols slung around their necks, the four Germans descended along the path to the door of the open burial chamber.

"This is a strange place," said Donkels. "A temple or, more likely, a grave. It's certainly not the sort of place you want to be entering at night, I'd have thought. These stone circles were made by people who believed in magic and witchcraft. And you desecrate a site like this at your peril."

"Donkels is right," said Hagen. "That's a grave in there. Best leave whoever it belongs to well alone, if you ask me."

"Nonsense," said Grenzmann. "It's perfectly obvious that they're hiding in here. Which means that this grave has already been desecrated. Not that it is of any concern to us. We're German soldiers, not a bunch of old women. It's just a question of going in here and getting them."

Corporal Hagen stared nervously into the entrance. A strange smell filled the air; he sniffed it suspiciously. "Maybe so," he said. "But sometimes old women know best. And it is very dark in there. Perhaps it would be better just to wait here until the morning. It couldn't do any harm, could it? If they are hiding in there, it's not like they can go anywhere else now, is it?"

"It might be a trap," suggested Donkels. "Suppose they're armed."

"Give me that flashlight," demanded Grenzmann, and stepped through the doorway.

Reluctantly, the three SS men followed him along a wide stone passage that turned to the left as it descended down a gentle slope.

"He doesn't lack courage," Hagen whispered to the other two. "I'll say that for him."

"Is that what you call it?" said Donkels. "If you ask me, he's going to get us all killed. I've got a funny feeling about this place. As a matter of fact, ever since we got started, I've had a peculiar feeling about this whole business. As if there was something not quite right about these wild horses and this child."

"Maybe there will be treasure," said Hagen, trying to look on the bright side. "Perhaps, like Heinrich Schliemann, we'll find the Ukrainian version of the treasures of Troy and all die rich men."

Talk of treasure lifted the hearts of the Germans for a moment.

"As long as we don't just die," said the third SS man. "Like Schliemann."

"Silence in the ranks," hissed Captain Grenzmann.

As the passage came to an end, he moved the beam of the flashlight from the floor to the roof, revealing a high, vaulted ceiling that was covered with paintings like the ones they'd seen back in the waterworks.

"What is this place?" breathed Hagen.

"These are the same paintings we saw back at Askaniya-Nova," said Donkels. "Aren't they?"

"Nonsense," said Grenzmann, and pointed the beam of the flashlight straight ahead of them into the thick darkness. "Those were much more recent. These cave paintings are the real thing."

Another, even stranger, sight met their widening eyes—so unutterably remarkable and unearthly that the Germans were stunned into silence as they tried to make sense of what they were looking at in the impatient beam of Grenzmann's flashlight.

The three SS men gasped, and even Grenzmann felt his jaw drop; all thoughts of the original objects of their pursuit were momentarily forgotten.

"Incredible," he said.

It was a life-sized war chariot that resembled an ancient exhibit in the world-famous Pergamon Museum in Berlin. The charioteer appeared to be a young female wearing a breastplate and helmet, with a spear in her hand, and she stood on a waist-high, semi-circular chariot that was well equipped with arrows and javelins. Two horses were hitched side by side by a yoke, and next to them stood an enormous hunting dog. But what made the chariot group so marvelous to the Germans was that it appeared to be mostly made of solid silver, and their fear now gave way to greed.

"Look at that," said Hagen. "Did you ever see anything so lovely? So magnificent?"

"It's silver," said Donkels.

"If it is," said Hagen, "we're rich."

As soon as Kalinka heard the throbbing and ominous sound of the German motorcycles on the hill outside the burial chamber, she knew exactly what to do. Having just woken up, she might almost have said the idea had come to her in a dream, except that she couldn't remember having dreamed about anything very much. She knew instinctively that it was a good idea; besides, what else could they do? Even so, explaining the idea to Temüjin and Börte required all her powers of diplomacy.

She stroked Börte's stiff mane for a moment and then scratched Temüjin's muzzle, which he seemed to like.

"Look, I know you're both wild horses and that you're not and never could be domesticated," she said. "And I know that both of you would run a mile rather than wear any kind of a harness. I respect your freedom to be different from other horses and to breed only with your own. But this is a good idea, and I know it can work. And I can't think of a better way of getting back at the men who shot your brothers and sisters at Askaniya-Nova than this, can you?"

Temüjin couldn't argue with her, nor could Börte; neither of the horses liked the idea of being yoked to the ancient chariot, nor did they care for being smeared with the silver paint the girl had found in a jar, but undeniably, the plan was a good one and stood a reasonable chance of success. All the same, wearing a harness went against everything that made the wild stallion what he was.

He was still thinking about Kalinka's argument when Börte nodded firmly and led the way to the chariot. Like any mare, she was always able to see reason before a stallion; but eventually Temüjin walked over and stood beside her. And patiently the two wild horses allowed themselves to be harnessed to the ancient chariot.

It was, Kalinka reflected, just like harnessing the big Vladimirs to her father's coal cart back in Dnepropetrovsk.

This process was quickly completed, after which Kalinka buckled on the warrior priestess's armor and daubed Taras and herself with more of the silver paint. The armor was lighter than she had imagined. The bronze helmet felt comfortable—it was even a good fit—and the breastplate could have been made for her. It was now clear to Kalinka that the warrior priestess was of an age and build that were similar to her own. Hoping that she wouldn't have to use it, she picked up the spear and held it at the ready, while with her other hand, she took hold of the ancient leather reins and prepared to greet their unwanted guests.

She could hear the Germans now and see a flashlight as they walked down the winding passage that led into the burial chamber.

"I don't have to tell you that they'll kill us all if they can," she whispered. "But if we can all just stand completely still until I give the word, I'm certain we'll give them the biggest shock of their lives since the Battle of Stalingrad."

As soon as the beam from the captain's flashlight touched Kalinka and the animals, the silver paint seemed to glow in the dark; when they started to laugh and to dance around the floor, Kalinka realized with grim satisfaction that the Germans believed she and the animals were made of real silver.

"We're rich," said Hagen. "Look at her. She's probably solid silver. She makes those treasures of Troy look like secondhand junk."

"Unbelievable," said Donkels. "There's enough silver in that charioteer to pay the whole German army."

"Then it's lucky for us they're not here." Hagen laughed unpleasantly. "More for the rest of us, eh, lads?"

"What do you think, sir?" Donkels asked Grenzmann.

"This does seem to change things," admitted Grenzmann.

"Steady," Kalinka murmured through clenched teeth as she waited for all of the Germans to emerge from the passage. She hoped there weren't any more of them aboveground, but if there were, she was ready to give them battle. Things weren't going to be like in the botanical gardens—not if she could help it. And the very thought of what had happened there made her angry now. So angry that she screamed what she thought was an ear-piercing war cry, and snapped the reins in front of her so that the two Przewalski's horses sprang forward and galloped straight toward the terrified Germans.

Extreme greed now gave way to abject terror as the shock of discovering their silver charioteer and her hunting dog were apparently alive caused the four SS men to turn and run for their lives. The last thing anyone saw clearly, before terror caused his trembling hands to fumble and then drop the flashlight, was Captain Grenzmann disappearing under the horses' hooves, and then the iron-bound wheels of the chariot, which left him bruised and bleeding on the ground for several minutes.

In their rush to escape the darkness, and screaming almost as loudly as the terrible warrior priestess in the chariot, Hagen and Donkels collided with each other before running straight into a wall, and managed to knock themselves out.

The fourth SS man fled in completely the wrong direction, tripped on the skeleton of a dead horse and then fainted with horror when, having found the flashlight on the floor, he managed to crawl on top of the mummified corpse in the center of the burial chamber.

Fortunately, the eyesight of Przewalski's horses is excellent—even in the dark—and Temüjin and Börte quickly found the path that led out of the burial chamber; seconds later, they were speeding out of the ancient doorway. Kalinka was more used to driving the coal cart than a chariot—it was the speed of the thing that took her breath away, and this lack of charioteering experience was the main reason why the girl allowed her left wheel to clip one of the vertical beams supporting the heavy stone lintel, which brought the whole edifice down in a loud crash of snow and dust and rock, sealing the entrance forever.

Taras barked his approval, and Kalinka brought the chariot to a halt next to the motorcycles near the top of the slope to look for more Germans. But there were none, so instead, she turned to survey the damage her chariot wheel had done to the ancient monument.

"I think it's going to take them a while to get out of there," said Kalinka, who had little appreciation of the enormous weight of the stone lintel.

Temüjin and Börte reared up on their hind legs and neighed triumphantly. They had a keener appreciation of the true fate that had met the four Germans.

"Whoa, steady," said Kalinka.

Still holding the spear, she climbed down off the chariot platform and stabbed all six tires on the two motorcycles and their sidecars, just in case the Germans managed to escape sooner than she imagined. Then she threw the keys away for good measure, after which she conducted a swift search of the two sidecars to look for anything useful she could steal.

Kalinka hooted with delight as she found several packets of sausage, groundsheets, some lighters, some pumpernickel bread and cheese, some cigarettes and matches, ammunition, a pair of clean socks, woolen mittens, a bottle of schnapps, a bottle of beer, several canteens of water, a bag of apples, a thermos flask of lukewarm coffee, some chocolate, a book by someone called Goethe, a scarf, a snood and an SS officer's cap.

"You wouldn't think you could get so much stuff in the sidecars of two motorcycles," she said. "There are more supplies here than in a salesman's suitcase."

There was even a compass.

She gave the apples and the beer to the horses and half of the sausage to Taras. Taras also took the hat, and for a while, he used it as a chew, which he thought was a poor substitute for biting one of the Germans. Kalinka put on the scarf, the snood and the socks, and crammed everything except the ammunition into a soldier's forage bag.

She got rid of the armor and the helmet, and with handfuls of snow, she washed the silver paint off herself and the animals, after which she was very glad of the mittens. Then she took a quick compass reading and pointed out the route.

"I think we'd better leave right now," she said, stepping back onto the chariot platform. "There may be more Germans around here. So the quicker we're away from this place, the better."

Kalinka took hold of the reins, snapped her team forward again, and soon the chariot was racing across the hard-packed snow.

THE CHARIOT WAS VERY old, and after the collision with the entrance, it quickly developed a bias to the left that periodically required Kalinka to pull the reins hard to the right in order to keep them running in a straight line; then the left wheel started to stray up and down the axle with a loud squeak that soon drove them mad. They kept the chariot rolling for most of the following morning and part of the afternoon, but as soon as they reached a country road, the chariot collapsed on the faster, harder surface. No one was injured, but a cursory inspection revealed that it would never drive again.

While she unharnessed the horses, Kalinka uttered a few silent words to the warrior priestess for lending her the chariot. It wasn't a prayer but more of a thank-you, as well as an apology for spoiling her grave, although Kalinka knew deep in her bones that, in the circumstances, the little priestess would hardly have minded.

"I don't know what we'd have done without you," she said quietly. "And I sort of feel that it was you who gave me the idea while I was asleep. Either way, I'll never forget you. Not if I live to be a hundred."

After that, Kalinka was obliged to ride again, for which Temüjin, at least, was grateful, as he didn't much care for the chariot harness. Running in a straight line and without accelerating ahead of Börte was as much discipline as he could endure for one day.

But before mounting Börte again, Kalinka put a folded groundsheet over the mare's back to cushion her against the girl's own weight, not that there was much of this; she was still very thin, much thinner than she'd been when living at home with her mother and father, when food was plentiful.

Kalinka remembered how she had always refused to eat her mother's borscht—she'd always hated beets.

"What wouldn't I give for a bowl of hot borscht now?" she muttered. "I'll never turn my nose up at food again—no matter what it is."

Kalinka took a reading with the SS compass, although now that they were on a road, it was easier to find their way, especially as the Germans had erected a helpful sign that said SOUTH and SIMFEROPOL.

"I suppose it will be all right to travel on the road," she said, "just as long as we get off it again if we hear any traffic coming. It wouldn't do to run into a German patrol. Or anyone else, if it comes down to it—experience has taught me not to trust any of the people in this part

219

of the world. Some of them are just as bad as the Germans, and we can't trust them to do anything but let us down. Most of them would betray us for a bowl of soup."

And this reminded Kalinka of something else her grandfather had often said: "Dear God, protect and keep our neighbors . . . well away from us."

Farther south, the winter snows had melted but the ground was still hard with frost, and the trees were full of little sparrows that Kalinka felt obliged to feed with crumbs of bread and tiny bits of fat from the German sausage, of which she knew they were fond. To her delight, some of the sparrows flew down from the trees and sat on the Przewalski's and pecked the ticks from their coats. They made an odd little party on the road to Simferopol: Kalinka in her silver-streaked Astrakhan coat, Taras, the two horses and a flock of small but noisy sparrows.

The birds were not the only things that were airborne in the blue Ukrainian skies. Once, they saw a lot of planes flying overhead like geese in formation, and she decided that they were probably bombers, but they were too high for Kalinka to make out if they were German or Russian. Not that it seemed to matter all that much one way or the other to her, and she found herself uttering another one of her dear grandfather's sayings: "If they're dropping bombs on top of you, what's the difference?"

"I seem to be thinking of Grandfather a lot today," she told Taras. "I suppose it's because I miss him so much."

Near a deserted village called Mayachka, Taras found

an old barn for them to sleep in, where the sparrows finally flew away. There was plenty of hay for the horses to eat and a trough of water, although Kalinka had to break the ice on the surface for them to drink from it. They spent a quiet and comfortable night but slept too long, as she had intended to be up before dawn so that they could slip away before anyone discovered them. They were exhausted after their long journey however, and by the time they were all awake, the sun was halfway up the sky and a thin woman with a dark, pinched face was standing in the doorway of the barn.

The woman wore a white head scarf, a thick, gray flannel blouse, a high-waisted skirt, a loose coat and tall boots, but none of these fitted her very well, as she was as thin as a beanpole.

"Who are you?" snarled the woman.

"Is this your barn?" asked Kalinka.

"Yes," said the woman. "What do you want here?"

"Then I'm sorry to intrude. I meant no harm. I thought the place was deserted. I can pay you for the hay that my horses have eaten, if you like. They were hungry."

"It's as good as deserted," said the woman. "Most of the men have run away. Or been killed. And the Germans have killed all our livestock for food, so you're welcome to the hay, as there are no animals to eat it anyway."

"You look pretty hungry yourself," said Kalinka.

"Hungry?" The woman uttered a contemptuous sort of laugh. "Starving is what we are, girl. Starving. But the

Germans don't care one bit. Nobody cares if we eat or what we eat. I used to be a schoolteacher. Can you imagine? Me. I used to read books. Now I'd probably try to eat a book if you gave it to me. Many's the night I've fancied eating a good cookbook. See this coat? This coat used to have buttons on it, but I took off all the buttons because they were made of bone and boiled them all to make soup. That's how hungry we are, child." The woman looked away and sighed. "There are so many such things we've had to do because we are hungry that it would make a statue weep with pity."

"I have a little piece of sausage left, if you'd like it?"

The woman looked at Kalinka with a sharp, suspicious glint in her eye, as if she thought Kalinka might be playing a cruel trick on her.

"Go on. You have sausage?"

"Just a bit."

"Give it to me."

Kalinka gave the woman the rest of their sausage from the forage bag, which the woman wolfed down in a matter of seconds; she felt hungry just looking at the woman.

Then the woman said, "Strange-looking horses. Are they yours?"

Kalinka thought it best to say that they were and that so was the dog.

"Been a while since we saw any animals, least of all horses around these parts," said the woman, licking her lips. "Not anymore. No horses, no cattle, no goats, no pigs, no sheep, not even a chicken. People ate what animals they still owned just to stop the Germans from eating them. Then when our animals were gone, we ate anything that moved: pigeons in the trees, rabbits in the field, squirrels, rats and mice, cats and dogs—you name it, we've eaten it. We've even eaten cockroaches. It's not a bad meal, a cockroach. Bit crunchy. There's a lot of protein in a cockroach. But that was a while ago. A long while ago. Since then, times have been hard. Very hard. We've been eating stale rice and grass mostly."

By now Kalinka was aware that the thin woman was looking at Temüjin and Börte in a strange way; Taras sensed it, too, and curled his long tail back between his legs.

"Would you like some bread?" she asked the woman.

"Bread? You have bread?"

Kalinka offered the woman a piece of pumpernickel, and she ate it with her eyes closed, emitting such groans of pleasure and satisfaction that it might have been supposed she was eating some rare delicacy like Russian caviar or boiled lobster.

"Oh," groaned the woman, "that's good. I've dreamed of eating bread like that again. Real bread, not the stuff we have here. That's not much better than sawdust. Scratch, we call it, because it's made from grass and what we can scratch from off the floor and the ground. But your bread was marvelous. Thank you. That was delicious. Almost as delicious as that sausage."

"I stole it from the Germans," explained Kalinka.

"Did you, now? You took a risk doing that, girl. Which means I'm taking a risk letting you stay here." She shrugged. "There was a time when they'd have shot us both just for eating a piece of stolen sausage."

"I'm sorry. I didn't mean to put you in any danger."

"But the Germans have helped themselves to all we have and moved on, to the south—on to the Crimean peninsula—so I suppose it's probably safe enough now. You're welcome to stay here as long as you want, girl. We've got nothing, but you're welcome to share it. Rest up awhile. You look tired. Eat all the hay that you want. You and your horses."

The thin woman waved at the barn and fixed a narrow smile on her pinched face.

"What's your name, child?"

"Kalinka. What's yours?"

"Suliko."

But because Suliko was the name of another Russian folk song, Kalinka assumed that the woman was just being sarcastic.

"No, really," said Kalinka. "It is Kalinka."

The thin woman sneered as if she didn't believe her. "Makes no difference to me what you're called," she said. "I'm sure I don't care one way or the other."

"And this is Taras," said Kalinka, pointing at the wolf-hound, whose ears were all the way back as if he didn't like the thin woman at all.

"Will you have some tea, child?" she asked Kalinka.

"Yes, please," said Kalinka. "If you can spare it."

"Tea is about all we do have." She nodded. "Well, you wait here and I'll go and fetch the samovar. There's no sugar, I'm afraid. Or jam to put in it." She laughed. "Just a tarnished-looking spoon."

Then she walked out of the barn, leaving Kalinka with a new dilemma.

"What she says sounds friendly enough, I suppose," she told Taras. "But there's something about her face and her manner that doesn't feel quite right and that I don't like. I'm not sure what it is, exactly. It's not that she said anything so strange. The war has been very hard on everyone. But it's just that she kept looking at you like you were her next meal, Taras."

Taras lay down and sighed. Was there no end to the savage cruelty that human beings were capable of?

"Look, you three, stay here. I'm going to follow her and see if I can find out if she really means that we should stay. Or if she's planning to sell us out to the Germans."

Kalinka peeked out of the barn and watched the woman crossing an empty field; she appeared to be in a hurry. The girl quickly followed her to a row of low wooden houses with thatched roofs that had seen many better days. Given what the thin woman had said, Kalinka wondered if she and her family might even have eaten some of the thatch. She crept up to the grimy window and looked inside. The walls of the house were almost as thin as the windows and Kalinka could hear everything that was said in the bare little room.

A bearded man wrapped in animal skins was sitting in front of a meager fire. The thin woman prodded him roughly and fetched a large cooking pot down from a hook on the ceiling.

"Here, Ivan Ivanovich, you'd better stir yourself," said the woman. "We've got guests."

"Guests? Here? What do you mean? Have the Germans returned?"

"No, thank goodness. We've seen the last of them, I think."

She drew open a drawer and handed the man a long knife, a hatchet and a sharpening stone.

"Now listen, I want that knife and that hatchet sharpened as quickly as possible."

"Why?" The man laughed a horrible sort of laugh. "Are you thinking of doing away with yourself, Anfisa Petrovna?"

"I knew her name wasn't Suliko," Kalinka whispered to herself.

"Very funny," said the thin woman. "Didn't you hear what I said, you miserable old goat? We've got guests. I just went into our barn and found more fresh food walking around in there than this whole village has seen in years: two horses, a dog and a girl—they're all hiding in there."

"You're seeing things," said the man in the chair.

"Hunger does that to you. You imagine things that aren't there. I swear, if you stare at this fire long enough, you'll see a side of beef on a spit."

"No, I'm not seeing things. They're there, all right. What's more, they're all in reasonable condition. The girl is thin, but there's still some meat on her bones. If we kill them all now, we can make enough sausage to last us right through until the summer."

The man stood up. If anything, he was even thinner than the woman—not much more than a living skeleton. "If you're not seeing things, then you're joking," he growled. "It's not possible. All of the fresh meat around here is gone."

"No, it's true, as I'm standing here now."

"Honest?"

"Real meat that's still breathing in our barn. All we have to do now is to butcher it."

"Then we're saved."

"Yes. We're saved."

"Horse is good," said the man. "Dog is better. But a girl is best. Just like pork, so they are."

He started to sharpen his hatchet, as ordered.

The woman laughed cruelly. "I told them they could stay as long as they want, but I think the girl was a bit suspicious of me. So we'd better do it tonight. When they're asleep."

"How will you cook them?"

"I'll use the horses for sausage meat, like I said. The

dog should make a nice roast. Several nice roasts. It's a big dog. And the girl—I was thinking—a tasty stew."

"Stew," said the man, and grinned horribly.

"What meat we don't use we can dry and use to make salted *bresaola*—so we can chew on something when the fancy takes us. Thank goodness there's still plenty of salt. From all the tears I've shed, I shouldn't wonder."

Kalinka had heard enough; she sprinted back to the barn, grabbed her forage bag and slung it over her shoulder.

"Come on. We're getting out of here."

Temüjin and Börte both climbed to their feet.

"I thought the Germans were bad," muttered Kalinka. "But these people are much worse. I suppose that this is what war does to people. It turns them into evil monsters."

Taras put down his chew and stood up.

"I just hope you've eaten lots of hay," Kalinka told the horses, "because we have to leave immediately. They're horrible people. Worse than you could ever imagine. They're actually planning to eat us. All of us. That's right, Taras. Me too. They're cannibals. I've heard stories about people like this. But I never really imagined they could be true. I knew that woman was looking at us in a strange way. I just wish I hadn't given her the last of our sausage and some bread."

Taras barked his agreement.

"To think I actually felt sorry for her."

Kalinka jumped up on Börte's back and rode quickly

out of the barn, with Temüjin and Taras following; in the distance, she could see the woman running after them. She was carrying a samovar on the end of a broom handle that was balanced over her shoulder.

"Wait, wait," shouted the woman. "You haven't had your tea."

Kalinka wheeled the mare around to take another look at the woman; she wanted to see if she and her husband were capable of mounting a pursuit.

"Fortunately for us, they're so starved that I don't think they have the strength to chase us," she said. "If they weren't so horrible, I might pity them both. A bit."

THEY GALLOPED FOR WHAT seemed like kilometers, across open fields and through dark forests with trees as tall as the tallest church steeple. After the frightening incident with the cannibals, Kalinka didn't have much to say to the others; in front of the dog and the horses, she felt ashamed that human beings could behave quite so badly to their own kind.

"I guess there's no accounting for what makes people do the things that people do," said Kalinka.

Taras barked in agreement.

The countryside here was badly scarred by war; everywhere there were broken tanks, ruined buildings and shell holes, abandoned artillery and discarded rifles, burning trucks and, on one occasion, a whole village that had been set ablaze.

"I think we must be getting nearer the Russian lines,"

she told her companions. But she neglected to mention to them that they would have to get through the German lines before they could reach their Russian ones; there seemed to be no point in worrying the animals unnecessarily.

Sometimes Kalinka also saw the bodies of dead men—both Russian and German—but she did not avert her gaze as her mother would probably have ordered. After what had happened to her family at the botanical gardens, nothing could have shocked Kalinka—not anymore. Besides, she knew that the dead—while not pleasant to look at—could do her no harm; it was the living you had to watch out for, as had been proved only too well by the cannibal couple of Mayachka.

Farther on, she saw patches of sand on the fields, and a number of times, she thought she could even smell the sea; then near a village called Novooleksiivka, she saw a rusting railway line and a stationary train consisting of what looked like empty boxcars. Thinking that they might rest in one of these—perhaps even travel in one—Kalinka climbed into a boxcar and opened the sliding wooden door so that the dog and the two horses could leap aboard beside her. She closed the door and shared what remained of their provisions with Temüjin and Börte and Taras; and after, she fell asleep.

When she awoke again, the train was moving.

Kalinka groaned, jumped to her feet but relaxed a little

when she saw that the train was clearly moving south; she took a compass reading to make sure, but she hardly needed to, since the railway track was on a bridge over water.

"That's either the Black Sea or the Sea of Azov," she told the others. "But I think the Sea of Azov is more probable, since we've been heading southeast since we left Askaniya-Nova. It's the shallowest sea in the world. And the river Don flows into it. I know that, because we did the Sea of Azov in geography, in my last term at school before the Germans arrived.

"Anyway, here's the plan: we'll ride this train until it gets dark and then we'll wait for it to slow down or stop, at which point we'll get off. We could walk, but why walk when you can ride? That's what I say."

Taras barked his agreement; his paws were sore and he was quite happy to lie down and let the train take the strain.

They hadn't traveled very far when some planes flew over at a very low altitude and they heard a series of deafening explosions. After calming the two horses—who'd never heard anything as loud as a bomb explosion—Kalinka opened the door of the boxcar and leaned out, only to see that the bridge behind them no longer existed; all that remained to indicate that it had once been there was a huge plume of smoke and pieces of wood that were still flying through the air.

"Oh my goodness," she said. "The planes bombed the

bridge. We were on that just a minute or two ago. We could have been killed."

She found it hard to decide if the bridge had been bombed by the Russians or the Germans, but the bombing of the bridge had the useful effect of making the train go faster. It soon became evident to Kalinka that it wasn't going to stop again until it reached its final destination.

"I expect the driver is a little nervous about stopping anywhere for very long after something like that," she said. "And I can't say I blame him. It seems as if you stand still long enough in this world, someone is sure to drop a bomb on you."

For a while after that, Kalinka kept a nervous eye on the sky by leaving the door open a crack, but before very long, the rhythmic movement of the train overtook her and she fell asleep again.

This time when she awoke, the train had stopped at a station in Simferopol, and hearing loud voices outside their boxcar and with her heart in her mouth, Kalinka peered through the slightly open door. A horrifying sight met her widening and fearful eyes: on the station platform were hundreds of German soldiers, and what was even worse, they looked as if they were preparing to get on her train.

"It's the Germans," she gasped. "What are we going to do?"

Taras licked her hand in a vain attempt to cheer her

up. Temüjin let out a heavy sigh and then flicked his tail irritably. Börte pressed her hot muzzle against Kalinka's ear and tried to breathe some encouragement into the girl, as if to say, "Don't be so hard on yourself. You tried your best."

"You're right," said Kalinka. "There's nothing we can do except wait for them to find us here."

She shook her head and stroked Börte's muzzle for a moment. In truth, since what had happened in the botanical gardens, Kalinka cared little for her safety; she had no illusions about what became of escaping Jews. But she felt that she had failed to carry out the very important task that Maxim Borisovich Melnik had given her: she had failed to save the last two Przewalski's horses in the world, because surely the Germans would kill them and eat them as the SS had killed and eaten all the others.

"I'm so sorry," she said, stroking Börte's head. "I've led you all to disaster, haven't I? Can you ever forgive me?"

She tried to put her arms around Temüjin's neck, but he pulled away and walked to the opposite end of the boxcar and stared at the wooden wall as if he couldn't bear to look at Kalinka. Like Kalinka, he had no illusions about the fate that awaited them all. But then Börte made an impatient snort at him that only a mare could make at a stallion, and remembering his manners, Temüjin turned to face the girl. He walked toward her, and this time he bowed his head in acknowledgment of all the enormous efforts she had made on their behalf.

The next second, the boxcar door was thrown open and the four intrepid travelers were faced with lots of large, red-faced German soldiers, all of them demanding loudly to know who she was and what she was doing on their troop train.

JOACHIM STAMMER WAS A captain from the Second Company of the German field police, whose headquarters were on Rosa Luxemburg Street, in a former Soviet NKVD building in the center of Simferopol, a major city on the Crimean peninsula. He was a professional policeman from the city of Bonn, where his parents and his wife still lived in a big house near the university where his father worked.

He was just about to go off duty when he received a telephone call from the local railway station to say that some soldiers had found a girl who had stowed away on a train that was detailed to take troops out of the besieged city to the coastal town of Sevastopol, for evacuation to Germany. The girl was Ukrainian, and there was talk that she might be a partisan fighter or a spy, so Stammer put on his helmet and greatcoat, and walked to the station, which was only a couple of hundred meters from his office. There was little point in using his car, as the roads were badly bomb-damaged; the city was now under constant attack from the Russian air force and could no longer be defended against the Red Army. Even as he picked his way among the bomb craters, a long-range artillery shell landed just across the Salhir River and exploded with a massive bang that shook the ground underneath Stammer's jackboots. The capture of the town of Simferopol by the Red Army could only be a matter of a few days now. The sooner the better, thought Stammer, because although he was a German, he was not and never had been a Nazi, and had not wanted to fight a war with Russia; all he wanted now was a chance to get home.

The railway station on Lenin Boulevard had once been an elegant white building that, with its clock tower and low Corinthian-columned arches, had resembled a church more than a railway station; but now it was little better than a ruin. He climbed over a pile of rubble and hurried inside as another artillery shell came whizzing overhead.

Partisans and spies were always shot, and Stammer hoped that the girl would turn out to be something else, as he had no appetite for handing her over to the SS. Even before he laid eyes on Kalinka, he was determined that he would do his best to make sure that this never happened. One way or the other, there had been much too much killing on the Eastern Front, by both sides, and Captain Stammer was hopeful of getting home without having anything bad on his conscience. Indeed, he now believed it was his mission in life to do one or two good things before the end of the war that might, in a very small way, help atone for some of the terrible things that the Nazis had done in the Soviet Union.

The station manager escorted Stammer to a railway siding where even now a train was being boarded by hundreds of German soldiers anxious to escape the constant artillery fire and falling bombs; near the end of the train was a boxcar guarded by two of his own men.

"The prisoner is in there?" he asked his sergeant.

"Yes, sir. Where we found her. We thought it easier to keep her in there because of the horses."

"Horses?"

"Yes. The girl has two horses with her. And a dog. She understands some German, I think—I'm not sure. I don't speak any Ukrainian, so there's not much I can tell you about her other than the fact that she's scared. Terrified."

"That's all right. I can speak quite reasonable Ukrainian."

"I also have a rather irate artillery lieutenant who's anxious to claim this boxcar for his men as soon as possible so that the train can get moving." The sergeant pointed down the platform, where an officer was now advancing toward them. "That's him there."

"All right, I'll handle him."

Stammer spoke to the lieutenant and assured him that

he could have the boxcar for his men just as soon as he had spoken to the prisoner.

"How long will that take?"

"A few minutes."

"This train has to get moving as soon as possible, sir," said the lieutenant. "It's a sitting duck for those Russian fighter-bombers as long as it's waiting in this station."

"Just let me do my job, Lieutenant."

Stammer opened the door of the boxcar and saw a frightened-looking girl, about fourteen years old, two nervous horses and an emaciated Russian wolfhound. The wolfhound growled menacingly. As soon as he clapped eyes on them, Captain Stammer realized what the girl was not—she was certainly no partisan fighter and probably not a spy. At the same time, he realized exactly what the horses were: Stammer's father, Wilhelm, was a doctor of zoology and natural history at the University of Bonn; Wilhelm Stammer was a world expert on freshwater snails and parrot fish. As a boy, Joachim had visited zoos all over Germany with his father, and in Berlin, he had once seen—and never forgotten—the rare Przewalski's horses.

"May I come in and talk with you?" he asked.

A little surprised that the German was so polite, Kalinka nodded and put an arm around Taras to restrain him from biting the man.

Captain Stammer climbed up and closed the boxcar door behind him.

"What's your name?" he asked.

"Kalinka."

"Well, Kalinka, we mean you no harm."

"I wish I could believe that."

"Really. It's all right."

"I don't care what happens to me, but please, you have to let these horses go. These are extremely rare Przewalski's horses. These horses go back tens of thousands of years. They're the horses on the paintings in the caves in France and just about the only living contact with our Stone Age ancestors."

"I know," said Captain Stammer.

"Przewalski's horses are extinct in all but name," Kalinka continued. "Which makes them extremely important. This is a breeding pair—possibly the last pair anywhere in the world. If just one of these two horses dies, it will be another dreadful crime in this dreadful war. They're not an inferior breed to domesticated horses, nor are they harmful to any other bloodline, because they actually prefer their own kind. But they are extraordinary and unique and extremely valuable. And I'll bet any zoo would pay big money to have animals like these."

"I know," said Captain Stammer.

"There were a lot more of them—perhaps as many as thirty—living north of here, but they were shot by your SS. I managed to rescue these two and ran away, hoping that I might find someone who understood the zoological importance of these animals. Someone who knows that the last two of anything in this world is like an extra special gift from Noah's ark. Someone who knows what happened to the dodo and to the woolly rhinoceros and to the *Sivatherium*."

"I know," said Captain Stammer.

Kalinka hesitated for a moment. "You do?"

"Actually, no, I'm not sure what a *Sivatherium* was," he admitted.

"Oh, it's a sort of cross between a giraffe and an okapi, I think."

Captain Stammer nodded. "Look, I'm sorry about the other horses. Very sorry, indeed. Not all of us Germans are like the SS, you know. Some of us are really quite civilized. As it seems are these horses. Which is to say that they don't seem to be all that wild."

"They're behaving themselves at the moment," she said. "They're usually as wild as the northeast wind."

"That's good."

"You mean—" Kalinka took a deep breath and tried to contain her emotion. "You mean you're going to help us?"

"I'll certainly do what I can," said Captain Stammer. "But it isn't going to be easy. In case you hadn't noticed, there's a war on. You have to understand that there's only going to be so much that I can do for these horses, and for you. Right now I need to get you off this train, but I don't want them charging up and down the platform. Someone—or they—might get injured."

"They'll behave, if I tell them."

"Excellent. There's a zoo here in Simferopol. On

Pushkin Street. I think the best thing would be if you were to go there and wait for your own people to turn up. It won't be long now before this whole city is overrun by the Red Army, and you can make your case for these horses to them. One more thing. Are you Jewish? Because if you are, under no account must you admit that if you're asked about it. Do you understand?"

"Er, yes, I think so."

"Is there anything on your person that might identify you as a Jew? A yellow star? Or a blue one? A number tattooed on your arm? A piece of jewelry?"

"No, nothing."

"That's good. If anyone asks, you are a Ukrainian peasant. And a good Christian. Understand?"

Kalinka nodded.

The captain smiled. "That goes for the horses, too," he said.

She realized he was making a joke, but she was still much too scared to smile back at the captain.

"Right, then. We'd best go. The zoo is about half an hour's walk south of here. But the city is under bombardment, so it could be a bit frightening for you and the horses. Not to say dangerous."

"We're used to danger," said Kalinka.

Stammer nodded. "Yes, I think you probably are."

It was, as the German captain had promised, a frightening walk to the zoo. Every so often, an artillery shell came whistling across the blue sky, but mostly the shells landed in the north of the city, and she and Captain Stammer reached the zoo without mishap.

"Of course, all or nearly all of the animals that were here are gone," he explained as they went through the zoo's main gate. "We couldn't spare the food to feed them, and I'm afraid we had to put many of them down. For someone like me, that's a very sad thing to see. I spent a lot of time in zoos when I was a boy. Which is how I come to know something about these horses, of course. Years ago, before the war, I saw the Przewalski's in the Berlin Zoo, you know."

The captain helped Kalinka find a suitable place to keep the horses; there was a paddock with plenty of grass, which, according to a sign on the fence, had previously been the home of some goats. Nearby was a birdhouse, where the captain suggested Kalinka might stay herself. He even told her some places she might try to scavenge some grain to feed the horses.

"Tomorrow, I'm being transferred to Sevastopol," he said. "But I'll try to look in again with some food for you and the dog before I go. After that, you'll just have to keep your head down and your fingers crossed until we've gone."

When he left, Kalinka looked at her three companions and shook her head. "Can we trust him, do you think?"

Taras, who had a dog's sense about the humans who could be relied on and those who could not, wagged his tail in the affirmative.

"Yes, I think we can," said Kalinka. "I mean, if he was going to turn us in, he'd have done it by now, right?"

Temüjin nodded gravely as if nothing more needed to be said. Humans continued to surprise him; they were much more unpredictable than the wildest horses.

"It's strange, don't you think?" said Kalinka. "That's to say, you get used to the idea that all Germans are horrible and then you meet one who seems very kind. All the same, I think we'll wait and see if he comes back with some food, like he said he would. We'll have a better idea of him then."

But the captain *was* as good as his word, and a couple of hours later, he was back with food, a blanket, a few candles, some Ukrainian newspapers, a couple of Russian flags, an encyclopedia, a steel helmet and a letter.

"The letter is written in Russian," he told her, "just in case the soldiers who liberate you don't understand Ukrainian. You should give it to whoever is in charge of this city after the Red Army takes over here again. And the encyclopedia has a very useful entry in Russian about the Przewalski's horses, which ought to help explain their zoological importance."

"And the helmet?"

"I advise you to wear it, of course. This bombardment is likely to get worse before it gets better. But make sure you take it off when the bombardment ends, and wave the red flag at your own people when they turn up. So they'll know you're friendly. Only please keep it hidden until we Germans have gone. Just in case."

"What will happen to you all when you get to Sevastopol?" she asked.

"That's a very good question." Captain Stammer sighed. "I really don't know. But to be honest, it doesn't look good for any of us. We're hoping to hold the Russians long enough to organize an evacuation by sea." He shook his head. "But it's going to be difficult without decent air cover. I've a feeling we've left it too late and that a lot of us aren't going to make it off this peninsula."

"I'm sorry," said Kalinka, who had a big heart and hated to hear of anyone who was in fear of his life—even German soldiers, but especially this particular German soldier.

"Don't be," he said. "It's good for you that we're going, for you and your country, too. This invasion was a terrible mistake. We should never ever have come here."

Kalinka nodded. This could hardly be denied, but it was good to hear a German who admitted as much. Captain Stammer was so different from Captain Grenzmann, she wondered that they could even be from the same country.

"Well, good luck anyway," she said. "And thank you. You've been very kind to me. And to the horses." Kalinka picked up her forage bag. "I have a present for you." She handed over the cigarettes and the bottle of schnapps she'd taken from the SS sidecar.

The captain stared at these gifts with amazement. "Schnapps," he said. "I don't believe it. I haven't seen a bottle of schnapps in ages. And cigarettes. Thank you, Kalinka."

"Don't mention it."

"Safe journey," he said. "Safe journey to you all. And goodbye."

After the captain had gone, Kalinka shook her head at their good fortune. And then she reread Max's letter, because the kindness she'd received from Stammer had reminded her of something the old man had said.

"Yes, it's true what you wrote, Max," she said. "Not all of the Germans are bad. If there are others as nice as that captain, then maybe there's hope for them yet. And perhaps not just for them, but for mankind in general."

Taras growled as if he wasn't sure about this. After what had happened to Max, he had badly wanted to bite a German soldier; any German soldier would have done, even a kind one.

Kalinka looked around and nodded with some satisfaction: Temüjin and Börte were eating the grass in their new enclosure, and already they looked to be completely at home.

"Well, this isn't so bad," she told Taras. "Could be a lot worse. I think our troubles might just be over."

But she was wrong.

THE FIRST RUSSIAN ARTILLERY shell landed in the zoo early the next morning while Kalinka was still asleep and badly damaged what had once been the zoo's ticket office. She put on her German steel helmet, hurried out of the birdhouse where she and Taras had spent the night, and went to see that Temüjin and Börte were all right, just as a second shell missed the zoo and landed in the soccer stadium next door, leaving a plume of gray smoke and dust as tall as a building. To her horror, both of the Przewalski's horses were gone from the goat enclosure.

Kalinka felt her heart skip a beat. "They must have run off somewhere," she said to Taras. "Looking for food, perhaps."

The dog barked back at her.

"Find them," she said urgently to Taras, who bounded off to look for his two friends.

The girl stared anxiously up at the sky as a squadron of single-engine planes appeared overhead. But they were not dropping bombs, and to her relief—at least until she remembered that Captain Stammer was probably going there—they seemed to be heading southwest, toward Sevastopol. But their presence underlined just how vulnerable the Przewalski's horses were in the zoo's open spaces.

"We need to find some sort of a bomb shelter," she told herself. "And quick."

Trying to contain her anxiety that something terrible had happened to the horses, Kalinka ran to search the zoo for a building with a basement; it was a good way of occupying her mind. But when she rounded the corner of the bear enclosure, a frightful sight met her eyes that made her worry even more.

For a brief second, she thought it was a large gray rock, but the smell of decay and putrefaction swiftly changed her mind.

Lying on the ground, inside what had once been its enclosure, lay the huge body of a dead elephant. It smelled even worse than it looked—so bad that Kalinka gasped and covered her nose and mouth. She wasn't sure if the poor animal had been killed by a bomb or by German soldiers who'd been unable to feed it, but either way, it was the saddest thing she'd seen since leaving Askaniya-Nova. Kalinka had never seen an elephant before, and it was a source of great regret to her that the first one she saw should also be dead.

There wasn't time to mourn the poor beast. Another shell zoomed over her head and landed harmlessly in a park to the west. She saw pieces of tree fly up into the air. Nowhere aboveground seemed safe from the Russian artillery. But a little farther on, she found what promised to be a good place of sanctuary, the zoo's aquarium.

Kalinka ran through the open door, past the cashier's window, and down a curving flight of stairs into an evil-smelling basement with blue mosaic walls and stone floors. Apart from the stink of fish, it seemed perfect. Passing through an arch that was painted to look like the open mouth of a whale, she flipped the electricity switch on the wall, without result, but there was at least some daylight coming through the top of the green fish tanks, most of which were thankfully empty of fish and water.

"This looks fine," she said. "With a few candles at night, we should be safe down here until the worst of the bombardment is over."

She hurried upstairs again, hoping that the wolfhound's keen nose would soon track her down and the dog would take her to the horses, or even better, bring them to her. And there was no time to lose; outside, she heard an explosion as another shell hit the soccer stadium. She might almost have pitied the Germans—at least Germans like Captain Stammer—who were the targets of such relentless bombardment.

In the damp shadows ahead of her, something moved and then growled, and Kalinka felt her blood run cold. She caught a faint glimpse of four legs and a whiff of something pungently musky and very much alive. At first, she thought it was a large dog, but when the animal growled again—a low, rumbling growl that was full of sharp teeth—Kalinka realized that this was not like any growling dog or wolf she'd ever heard before; it was something else. She backed away, retreating down a few of the stairs that led to the basement, as she guessed that the animal was now between her and the front door. She knew that if she made a run for the outside, the animal would certainly attack.

Glancing around for some kind of weapon, Kalinka saw that at the bottom of the stairs was a cone-shaped fire extinguisher. Quickly she turned and ran downstairs, and fetched the extinguisher off the wall. But it was heavy.

In the shadows, the animal growled again, and this time she thought it sounded more like a lion than a dog—a lion that had escaped from its ruined enclosure, perhaps.

Kalinka started slowly up the staircase, and at last, she saw what she was up against. The animal had a short tail and pointed ears, with big padded paws and goldish fur with brown spots, and for a moment, she thought it was a leopard before she recognized that it was actually a very different kind of big cat: it was a lynx. It was over a meter long and at least half a meter high at the shoulder; she estimated that the lynx probably weighed as much as thirty kilograms. It might have been bigger if it hadn't been so thin; like everything else in that part of the world, the cat was hungry—hungry enough to consider eating Kalinka.

The lynx crept toward the top of the stairs, crouched down as if preparing to spring and then growled again; only this time, the cat showed her its teeth and its claws as if to remind her that it was strong enough to bring down a fully grown deer, which was its normal prey. Kalinka lifted the extinguisher and prepared to hit the plunger, but since it was full of water, it took all of her strength to aim the nozzle at the cat.

She was just about to fire a jet of water at the lynx when she heard a bark. It was Taras, and Kalinka would have cheered if she hadn't feared for the wolfhound's chances, because a hungry lynx was a formidable opponent for a dog, even a dog as large as Taras. The lynx turned abruptly and, snarling fiercely, sprang at him.

Kalinka ran up the stairs two at a time to find Taras locked in a vicious battle with the big cat. Taras had a good grip on the lynx's neck with his strong jaws, but the big cat was clawing his sides fiercely—so fiercely that each rake of its claws tore into the dog's fur.

Kalinka screamed with anger and leapt to the dog's defense. "No, you don't!" she yelled at the lynx.

Now that she wasn't coming up the stairs, she no longer had to lift the nozzle of the heavy extinguisher so high, and Kalinka had a much better shot. Hoping to drive the big cat off, she fired a jet of water at both the animals, since it was almost impossible to tell them apart.

The cat let go of Taras immediately and twisted away, its face and thick fur dripping with water. The pointed ears looked like little black darts on the lynx's head. It stared balefully at the girl and then at Taras as the dog snapped at its heels before it bounded out of the aquarium door, with Taras giving chase to the lynx's short black tail.

Kalinka went outside and saw the lynx as it ran up a tree and, along the roof of one of the animal enclosures before it disappeared; but much more importantly, she saw Temüjin and Börte, who were standing in front of the door to the aquarium.

"Where did you two get to?" she asked. "I was worried about you both. Did the bombs scare you? I don't blame you for running away. I'm kind of scared myself. I never heard such an almighty racket."

Kalinka ran to the horses and stroked them affectionately, but as Taras returned from giving chase to the big cat, there was no time for an extended reunion; already she could hear another shell on the way, and without further delay, the girl led the dog and the horses into the aquarium and down to the basement. The two Przewalski's clattered down the stairs as if they'd been doing it all their lives.

Temüjin snorted loudly and trotted the length of the aquarium as if keen to inspect his new surroundings; Börte peered through the glass of one of the tanks and licked it experimentally and then kept doing it: the glass was covered in salt, and if there's one thing of which wild horses are fond, it's a delicious salt lick.

"All right," Kalinka told them. "You three stay down

here. I'm going back up to the birdhouse to fetch our supplies. You too, Taras."

Taras barked, and lying down on the floor, he began to lick himself. For a dog, there's almost nothing that tastes better than that.

She patted the dog fondly on the head, briefly inspecting him for signs of damage: one of his ears looked a bit ragged, but otherwise he appeared to be unscathed. Just then another bomb outside rocked the building they were in, showering them with dust and causing Kalinka to cover her own head and ears.

"That sounded too close for comfort," said Kalinka. "But I think we'll be safe enough down here."

UNDER CONSTANT BOMBARDMENT FROM the Soviet
Red Army, Kalinka and the cave horses and Taras
the dog spent a nerve-wracking night down in the abandoned aquarium of Simferopol. There was little chance of
anyone sleeping. Kalinka lit one of the candles Captain
Stammer had given her and let it burn all night; she decided that if she was going to be killed by Russian bombs,
she preferred that it should happen in the light than in
the dark. Temüjin and Börte lay on one of the SS groundsheets and did their best to ignore the terrifying noise.
Kalinka lay on another groundsheet and did the same.
But it wasn't just the noise that kept them awake; it was
hard to breathe, too. Each time a shell or a bomb landed
on the ground above, the impact sent clouds of dust into
the fetid air of the aquarium, and sometimes pieces of ce-
ment and mosaic fell onto their heads. On more than one

occasion, there was so much dust falling off the ceiling that it extinguished the candle; once, the glass of one of the fish tanks cracked loudly, and it was fortunate there was no water in it, or otherwise the floor would have been inundated. Several times, Kalinka screamed out loud with fright and covered her ears against the blasts, which did nothing to settle the nerves of Temüjin and Börte. The two horses lay close together, with the stallion's head laid protectively over the mare's neck, like two fond lovers, and if they all hadn't been subject to a harrowing ordeal, Kalinka would have felt more touched by the sight. But as things were, she was terrified—more terrified than she had ever been in her life. Even the arrival of the SS in Dnepropetrovsk had been less terrifying than the constant bombardment. She wrapped herself in the blanket, and for a while, she tried to read one of the newspapers, but mostly she just covered her ears against the terrible noise. Kalinka thought that it was like being inside an enormous metal box that someone was hitting with a sledgehammer again and again and again.

After some time, she tried to steel her nerve by counting the explosions, but she gave up when she reached a hundred.

"They have to stop soon," she shouted. "Surely they'll run out of shells."

But they didn't.

Kalinka couldn't have known it, but the Russians were firing Katyusha rockets at Simferopol; nicknamed

"Stalin's organ pipes," the rocket launchers were mounted on trucks and could fire four rockets a time and from a distance of more than five kilometers. The effect on the city was devastating.

Only Taras seemed able to tolerate the noise. He lay quietly next to Kalinka as if not in the least bit concerned about anything; she badly wanted to hug him to her for comfort, but she didn't, forbidding herself this selfish comfort in the hope that the brave wolfhound might get some much-needed sleep. Börte even came over and had a look and a sniff at Taras, as if envious of the wolfhound's extraordinary ability to relax.

At least that's what Kalinka thought.

"Shh," said Kalinka. "Don't wake him, Börte. He's tired. We're all exhausted. But him especially. You should have seen him fighting that lynx. You would have thought that the poor cat was a German officer, he was so fierce in attack."

But a little later on, she noticed that Taras was breathing strangely, as if he was nervous after all, and when she stroked the dog in an effort to calm him, she discovered that he was covered in something sticky.

"Hey," she said, "what have you been rolling in, you silly dog?"

Kalinka brought the candle close to the wolfhound to see what was on his coat and learned, to her horror, that Taras was covered with blood. And when she lifted the candle over him to inspect the dog more closely, she found that he was lying in a pool of his own blood. During the fight with the lynx, the wolfhound's sides had apparently been raked to the bone by the cat's powerful claws and he was now in danger of bleeding to death.

"I'm such an idiot," said Kalinka. "I should have taken a closer look at you after your fight with the lynx. Do you forgive me, Taras?"

Weakly, the wolfhound lifted his head for a moment, and with a faint wag of his curved tail, he licked the girl's face fondly.

"I have to do something," she told herself. "But what?" Desperate to help the stricken dog, she rummaged through her forage bag for something that might help, but there was nothing that seemed likely to do the job of fixing up an injured dog. What Taras needed most was a vet, but finding one in Simferopol was out of the question. Kalinka thought for a minute; she knew she'd seen a medical kit somewhere in the zoo, but where?

"Yes, I remember now. There was a first aid kit on the wall of the ticket office, wasn't there? Look, hold on, Taras. I'm going to fetch that kit. I'll be as quick as I can, all right?"

She grabbed her helmet and went up the stairs, where she peered cautiously out of the front door. Already the zoo looked very different from even a few hours before— the birdhouse was completely destroyed, and the dead elephant's enclosure was missing two of the walls. Even the dead elephant had disappeared. She had to look hard before she could even make out where the ticket office had been. Finally she saw the place and started to run.

The air was thick with the smell of cordite, burning wood and blasted stone; the monkey house was on fire, and it was fortunate that there were no monkeys in it. She could actually taste explosives on her tongue as she made her way through the bomb-damaged zoo. At any moment, a shell might have landed and blown her to pieces, but Kalinka's fear for the dog was greater than her fear for herself.

Close to the ticket office, she paused briefly beside an open cage with a sign hanging upside down on one screw that identified the enclosure as that of a Eurasian lynx (*Lynx lynx*).

"Well, that explains that," she muttered. "We were in his territory, I guess."

The sign also pointed the way to the lion house; somewhere, at the back of her mind, she hoped a small hope that the lynx was gone and that there would not be a lion loose in the zoo as well, but all that really mattered now was quickly finding that first aid kit and helping Taras.

This brief pause in front of the lynx enclosure almost certainly saved Kalinka's life.

She never heard the Katyusha rocket that hit the nearby lion enclosure, and she didn't hear anything for several minutes after that; all she knew was that she was lying down on the ground and staring up at the stars.

"Oh, I never realized," she heard someone whisper. "I

never realized how beautiful the stars are in the Crimea. There's the North Star, just where it ought to be. And look at that purple sky. It must be that we're so near the Black Sea."

It was a minute or two before Kalinka realized that the voice she could hear above the whistle in her ears was her own.

She swept some rubble off her chest, picked herself up and, feeling a little faint, knelt again for another minute until her head had properly cleared. Tasting blood, she spat and then wiped her mouth; her lip was cut, but that seemed to be her only injury. Her coal scuttle–shaped helmet now felt different against her head, and taking it off for a moment, she saw that there was now an enormous dent in the gray metal, as if something hard had hit it. Realizing just what a narrow escape she had experienced, Kalinka whistled with wonder.

"That was close," she said. "Any closer and I'd have been strawberry jam."

She put the helmet back on, tightened the chin strap as much as she could—it was too big for her, of course—and carried on to the ticket office.

There she found the door and one of the walls standing and not much else. Fortunately, the wall that was still standing was the one with the first aid kit on it. Kalinka opened it up and inspected the contents; there was iodine, bandages, surgical dressings, scissors, tape—there was even a needle and some suture thread.

"Yes!" she said triumphantly. "This is just what I need."

She lifted the box off the wall and ran back to the aquarium. Kalinka had seen her mother stitch her father's arm once, after he'd fallen off the coal cart, and thought she could probably do the same with the dog's wounds; she'd have to trim some of his fur and then cover the wound with iodine, which would sting, of course, but she felt Taras was brave enough to deal with that. In fact, she was sure she'd never met a more courageous animal than him.

Kalinka could tell something was wrong as soon as she was back in the aquarium. Taras had not moved from where he lay on the floor, but Temüjin and Börte were both standing beside him and the stallion was trying to move the dog gently with his nose. The dog did not stir, and what was worse, his long pink tongue was hanging out of his mouth.

Kalinka ran to his side, threw away her helmet, lit another candle and pressed her face close to the dog's chest. But it was too late. Taras was dead.

"Oh no," she said quietly. "Not you, too, you wonderful old dog. Not you, too."

She sat with the dog's noble head in her hands, but still she did not cry. How could she cry for a dog when she had not yet cried for her mother and father, her grandparents, her great-grandmother, her brothers and sisters, her aunts and her uncles, her cousins and her neighbors? How could she cry for Taras when she had not cried for

Max? Where was grief to be found for a wolfhound when there had been none for them? Somehow it would have seemed disrespectful to her family and to the old man to have wept for this brave and faithful dog when she had not yet stopped to weep for them.

Kalinka wrapped her friend's body in one of the German groundsheets and stitched it up carefully, so as to prevent some animal from eating him; then she dragged Taras to a far corner of the aquarium, where she had lit a special candle, and sat there in silent contemplation of his courage and his devotion.

"I shall miss you, dear Taras," she whispered. "You were faithful unto death. There never was a better dog than you. Not ever. Dear Max would have been so very proud of you."

After a moment—and quite unbidden—the two Przewalski's horses came and stood on either side of the dog's body and, in spite of the terrible noise of the continuing bombardment, would not leave, like an honor guard for a fallen comrade.

IT WAS A LITTLE before dawn when the Russian artillery bombardment finally ended and Kalinka and the cave horses could leave the aquarium and return to ground level and breathe some fresher air. Not that it seemed all that fresh. The lion house was still burning, and Kalinka had the thought that perhaps the bodies of some dead animals were being consumed by the flames; at least, she hoped that they were dead. A thin haze of gray smoke hung over everything like a fog, and pieces of ash were floating through the air like gray snowflakes.

An eerie quiet had descended on the city of Simferopol. After the death of Taras, Kalinka decided that she needed to be on her own for a while and so she left the horses to go and see if she could scavenge some more food. She thought it better that the horses remain at the zoo; she knew that if the bombardment started again,

Temüjin and Börte were intelligent enough to find their way back down to the makeshift shelter that was provided by the aquarium. Besides, there was still plenty of good grazing in the goat enclosure and the horses were hungry.

According to one of the newspapers she'd read, it was April, but things didn't feel much like spring as it was still very cold—probably because they were so close to the sea. The wind was still arriving from the northeast, with just a bit of sleet to make life hard for everyone.

She walked all the way back to the railway station and found the city deserted; the Germans were gone, but as yet there was no sign of the Russians. The city of Simferopol was ruined: the nearby velodrome was cratered like the surface of the moon, and a green church had a large, unexploded bomb sticking out of a wall. Most of the buildings had collapsed or were in a state of near collapse. With a few of them, whole walls had disappeared, revealing everything inside the houses—furniture, pictures, carpets—as if some careless giant ape had opened them up to look inside. Kalinka had not seen the movie *King Kong* herself, but she knew what it was about.

In a bakery shop near the central railway station, she found a couple of stale loaves and put them in her forage bag. In another shop, she managed to get a can of condensed milk. Then she went back to the zoo, where the Przewalski's horses were waiting patiently for her return. She split one of the loaves into two for them, before eating some of the other loaf herself and drinking the condensed milk, which tasted delicious.

Not long after her meal, the sun came out again and she heard the sound of music on a loudspeaker and instantly recognized "The Internationale"—which was a patriotic song the Russians were always playing.

"It sounds like the Red Army is here at last," she told the horses. "We'd better make you look like good Russian horses."

So she draped a red flag over each horse, and while Börte, who was used to having the groundsheet on her back, was able to tolerate this, Temüjin was not and kept tugging the flag off with his teeth.

"This is for your own good, you know," she told him, trying again and then again. "In case someone decides to make you their next meal."

But Temüjin kept pulling the flag off and dropping it on the ground. Finally, Kalinka decided to hang the flag on their enclosure, which seemed like the best alternative.

Red Army soldiers appeared in the zoo toward the end of the afternoon; they wore brown tunics and blue trousers and were very dirty, and regarded Kalinka with some suspicion.

"What are you doing here, child?" asked one, a Ukrainian.

"Waiting for you," she said. "My name is Kalyna Shtern, but everyone calls me Kalinka, like the song. I'm from Dnepropetrovsk, where the Germans killed all my family. I'm the only one left."

"Sorry to hear it," said the Ukrainian soldier, although he didn't sound very sorry at all.

One of the other soldiers was laughing and talking in Russian; he was looking at the horses, and although Kalinka couldn't understand everything he said, he seemed to be suggesting that he could eat a horse and probably would.

"No!" she yelled. "These horses are all the family I have now. They're very special wild horses from the Soviet People's Sanctuary Park at Askaniya-Nova. Przewalski's horses. All of their brothers and sisters were killed by the Germans, too; that means they're the last of their kind and very probably the rarest horses in the world. They're the same horses that you can see in cave paintings in France. Look, you'll understand more when you read this letter and the entry in this encyclopedia."

"Askaniya-Nova? That's two hundred kilometers from here," he said, sneering with skepticism. "Do you expect me to believe you walked all that way with two wild horses?"

"It's true, I tell you," she insisted.

"I don't have time for your fairy stories, girl," said the Ukrainian soldier, and unslinging his machine gun from around his neck, he walked toward the Przewalski's horses. "Sorry, but I've got hungry men to feed. Those two horses of yours will feed a whole platoon." He laughed. "Besides, your encyclopedia is no good to me. I can't read."

He aimed his machine gun at Temüjin, but Kalinka ran in front of the stallion and held out her arms as if she hoped to shield the horses from the Red Army soldier's bullets.

"Are you mad, child? Get out of the way before you get hurt."

"If you shoot them, I swear you'll have to shoot me first."

"Move, I tell you. My men's stomachs are more important than your pet horses."

"No, they're not," she insisted, and as if to emphasize the point, she jumped onto Börte's back. "Not this time. Don't you understand? These horses are one of the things you've been fighting for. They're an important part of what makes Ukraine and Mother Russia what they are. You kill them and you're destroying your own great victory here. I didn't walk all that way and endure the cold and beat off attacks by wolves, the SS, even cannibals, just so that you could fill your belly with some fresh meat, Comrade."

Reluctantly, the soldier lowered his weapon.

Impressed by Kalinka's courage and perhaps a little persuaded by the red flag that she had now draped over her own shoulders, the soldiers decided to fetch an officer to listen to her story and to determine the fate of the two Przewalski's horses.

The officer was a handsome man—a tall Russian major, wearing several medals on his tunic, who spoke good Ukrainian.

He listened patiently to the whole of Kalinka's story, glanced over the entry in the encyclopedia and then asked to read the German officer's letter.

She handed him the letter, which he took and read with more than a little curiosity; it was the first time since the start of the great patriotic war that he had ever had any communication with a German. Much to his surprise, the German's Russian was as courteous as it was good, and the letter affected him more than he could have explained.

To the Red Army officer now in charge of
  Simferopol
From Captain Joachim Stammer, of the German
  field police

Much respected sir,
  Against all the rules of war, I felt compelled to risk the displeasure of my own superior officers and write to you on behalf of Kalinka and her cave horses. I believe she has had a truly remarkable journey to try to bring them to safety. It remains to be seen just how rare these horses are; however, when I was a boy, I saw a small group of these animals in Berlin and my zoologist father

told me that there were perhaps only three dozen of them left anywhere in the world. Certainly that number must be much lower today. And it may actually be—as Kalinka herself will tell you—that this breeding pair is the last, which makes them virtually priceless.

The history of Przewalski's horse is an extremely difficult one to trace, not least because these horses—a true species of the Russian and Ukrainian steppes and the only species of true wild horses in existence anywhere on earth—go back thousands of years, certainly beyond the last ice age around ten thousand years ago. Some sources estimate the horses were running around this part of the world as long ago as 70,000 BC. But they are, without question, the same horses that can still be seen painted on the walls of caves all over Europe and, as such, they represent an almost unique connection with the very beginning of human history.

History will show that the invasion of your country by mine was a terrible crime, which I, for one, sincerely regret; for that unpardonable crime, I would ask you to accept my own sincere apology. If I were with you now, I would tell you that many Germans are not Nazis, and that, one day, we will try to make it up to you, after which, hopefully, our two countries will be friends again.

Much more importantly, however, I would also ask you to take steps to ensure the preservation of these unique animals, not just for Kalinka's sake, but for the sake of peace-loving men and women everywhere. Tomorrow's world will be a lesser place without Przewalski's horses. But I hope you will also agree that it is already a better place if the future lies in the hands of courageous children like Kalinka. As a citizen of the Soviet Union, you should feel very proud of her. As proud as I am to have known her, albeit briefly.

Yours sincerely,
Stammer, J., Captain
2nd German Field Police

The Russian major read the letter again and swallowed a lump in his throat, for he was very moved by the German captain's honest words.

Meanwhile, more and more Russian soldiers were arriving in the zoo, and Kalinka noticed that a few were carrying not just guns but balalaikas and accordions. Russian soldiers often took musical instruments with them when they were fighting. It was, she thought, a good sign when soldiers were carrying musical instruments.

"This German captain," the Russian major said to Kalinka. "What was he like?"

"Handsome, sir. Perhaps a bit like you, but younger. And kind, sir. Very kind. He risked his life to bring us here to safety. He wasn't the same as other Germans I've met. And I like to think there are more like him, somewhere."

"What happened to him?"

"He was evacuated to Sevastopol," she answered. "Although to be honest with you, Major, he didn't seem to think much of his chances for survival."

The Russian major nodded. "No. Nor do I. It's going to be bad there, too. But I'll say this for him: he writes a good letter. Don't worry, Kalinka. I will make sure that nothing happens to these Przewalski's horses. I give you my word on this. They're both quite safe now. I will assign them a personal bodyguard this very minute and make sure they are properly fed."

He reached up and lifted Kalinka down from the horse's back and stroked her cheek. Then he spoke to his sergeant.

"These horses are to be guarded night and day," he said. "Under no account are they to be harmed. Understood?"

"Yes, sir," said the sergeant.

"Thank you," she whispered.

"You look as if you could use a good meal yourself, not to mention a bath and a proper bed."

Kalinka nodded, and for no reason that she could think of, she started to cry. All of the emotion that had been bottled up inside the girl for months came spilling out; it was almost as if she had needed to feel safe before she could do this properly. And Kalinka wept like the Dnieper River would have if the Zaporizhia Dam had been destroyed. She wept as if the ground needed the moisture from her tears. She wept for her family, and she wept for Max, and she wept for Taras, and she wept that perhaps at last her sufferings were over.

The Russian major took the girl in his arms for a moment and held her trembling body close to his own.

"Hey, no tears," he said. "You're safe now. You and your cave horses. What's more, we've just won a victory here. And so have you. A great victory. You did something really important, Kalinka." He smiled and wiped the tears from the girl's eyes. "Tell me, child, how on earth did you come to have a name like Kalinka?"

"My real name is Kalyna. But my father used to call me Kalinka, like the song. He used to say I was as sweet as a snowberry—as a *kalinka.* And it sort of stuck. Everyone calls me Kalinka." Kalinka swallowed. "Or at least, everyone did."

"Is that so?"

The Russian major looked at his men. They were exhausted from many weeks of combat, and in spite of the victory at Simferopol, he knew their morale was low. But he was a clever man and knew a good thing when he saw it. Almost immediately, he realized that Kalinka was the answer to his own prayer as to how he was going to lift the spirits of his men to keep fighting until the last German had been expelled from Mother Russia and the great victory was assured.

"Well, then, Kalinka, the men of the Red Army love to sing. And I think 'Kalinka' must be just about our most favorite song." He turned to address his men with a grin on his face. "Isn't it, men?" He raised his voice. "Listen to me, Comrades. This girl here is a real hero of the Soviet Union. She may not wear a uniform or a medal, but she's as close to a genuine hero as any of us are likely to meet. She's traveled hundreds of kilometers to save these very rare wild horses. The little heroine's name is Kalinka."

"Kalinka!"

The news that the little heroine's name was Kalinka had an electrifying effect on the Red Army soldiers, who were increasing in number all the time. Many of them wanted to touch her because they were simple men and believed that some of Kalinka's luck might perhaps rub off on them like magic dust and keep them alive for the rest of the war. And who is to say they were wrong? Even Kalinka recognized that she was very lucky to be alive. Some of the soldiers patted her fondly on the head, others squeezed her hands and pinched her cheeks, and one or two felt moved to hug her or even kiss her nose and her ears and her mouth. There were so many soldiers around her that Kalinka was in danger of being squashed, which was why two of the men lifted her up on their big shoulders to help show her off to the rest of the men. But not before the major had tied the flag around her neck so that it would not fall off.

"So how about we sing to her and cheer her up, Comrades?" said the major. "How about we sing her our favorite song? How about we show her what we think of a real hero?"

This drew a loud shout of approval, although in truth he hardly had to ask his men. The Red Army never needed much of an excuse for a song and dance to keep up their spirits. Polished triangular balalaikas were already being tuned, bulky piano accordions were being buckled onto broad chests and shiny tin harmonicas were searching for middle C. To Kalinka, it all looked and sounded utterly chaotic until, as one man, the army fell silent and, almost imperceptibly, a single note began in the chests of the men like the hum of a huge swarm of honeybees. Gradually, this eternal note gathered in strength until it filled the Black Sea air in a great crescendo of male voices that sounded as if they were nothing less than a heavenly choir. The magnificent sound—for so Kalinka thought it—began and ceased and began again, glimmering and vast, an ebb and flow of both melancholy and joy that seemed to sum up everything the girl had been through; if men could produce such honey-sweet music with what was in their hearts, then surely there was still some hope for the world. And while nothing was or ever could be forgotten, Kalinka could now perceive some idea of a tomorrow for herself, too, not perhaps as the heroine of the steppes—as she had already heard herself described by some of the more poetically-minded soldiers—but as an ordinary Ukrainian woman.

And when they had finished singing "Kalinka," they sang it again, just because they could.

Kalinka looked over at the two Przewalski's horses, who were now grazing in their enclosure under an armed guard; Temüjin and Börte appeared to be quite oblivious of the song and its meaning, not to mention their improved status in the unpredictable world of men, which was exactly how it should have been, she thought. They were wild horses, after all.

Then she looked up at the sky above what remained of Simferopol's zoo. The acrid gray smoke of the Red Army bombardment had cleared from the sky, which was as bright a shade of Ukrainian blue as she had ever seen, to reveal a bright, hot sun that warmed Kalinka's cold face and seemed to thaw both it and her emotions, until at last, for the first time in almost a year, Kalinka found that she could smile again.

Her smile drew a cheer from the soldiers, and quickly turned into a grin and then laughter.

"Max," she whispered into the wind. "We made it. The horses are here with me. We're safe. At last, we're safe."

AUTHOR'S NOTE

Hear Russia's great Red Army Choir sing "Kalinka" here:
http://www.youtube.com/watch?v=3PkXpCsgj5U

"Kalinka" might be the best-known Russian song of all time. It is certainly the most popular. Some people think it's a folk song that's been around for a very long time. But it was actually written as recently as 1860 by the composer and folklorist Ivan Petrovich Larionov. With its speedy tempo and lighthearted lyrics, the song celebrates the snowball tree, a popular ornamental. But the actual content of the song is difficult to translate, as it contains many Russian expressions and words that hold a double meaning.

These are the words to "Kalinka":

Kalinka, kalinka, kalinka moya!
V sadu yagoda malinka, malinka moya!
Akh, pod sosnoyu, pod zelenoyu,
Spat' polozhite vy menya!

Ay-lyuli, lyuli, ay-lyuli, lyuli,
Spat' polozhite vy menya.
Kalinka, kalinka, kalinka moya!
V sadu yagoda malinka, malinka moya!
Akh, sosyonushka ty zyelyenaya,
Nye shumi zhe nado mnoy!
Ay-lyuli, lyuli, ay-lyuli, lyuli,
Nye shumi ty nado mnoy!
Kalinka, kalinka, kalinka moya!
V sadu yagoda malinka, malinka moya!
Akh, krasavitsa, dusha-dyevitsa,
Polyubi zhe ty menya!
Ay-lyuli, lyuli, ay-lyuli, lyuli,
Polyubi zhe ty menya!
Kalinka, kalinka, kalinka moya!
V sadu yagoda malinka, malinka moya!

Little snowberry, snowberry, snowberry of mine!
Little raspberry in the garden, my little raspberry!
Ah, under the pine, the green one,
Lay me down to sleep,
Rockabye, baby, rockabye, baby,
Lay me down to sleep.
Little snowberry, snowberry, snowberry of mine!
Little raspberry in the garden, my little raspberry!
Ah, little pine, little green one,
Don't rustle above me,

Rockabye, baby, rockabye, baby,
Don't rustle above me.
Little snowberry, snowberry, snowberry of mine!
Little raspberry in the garden, my little raspberry!
Ah, you beauty, pretty maiden,
Take a fancy to me,
Rockabye, baby, rockabye, baby,
Take a fancy to me.
Little snowberry, snowberry, snowberry of mine!
Little raspberry in the garden, my little raspberry!

ASKANIYA-NOVA

The nature reserve at Askaniya-Nova, in Ukraine, still exists and is open to the public.

Przewalski's Horse Today

All of the world's Przewalski's horses are descended from just nine of thirty-one horses in captivity at the end of the Second World War in 1945. And these same nine horses were themselves descended from approximately fifteen captured around 1900. A few Przewalski's horses have been successfully reintroduced to their native habitat, the steppes of Mongolia, and as of 2011 there is an estimated free-ranging population of over three hundred in the wild. The total number of these horses, according to a 2005 census, was about fifteen hundred.